This is ex-teacher Sue Hampton's sixth novel for Pegasus. Her love of music, art, dance, flowers and the natural world find expression in all her stories. Sue believes in the power of words and ideas and hopes her books will make readers think and feel.

Sue enjoys visiting schools and libraries to inspire young people to read and write good stories.

The Waterhouse Girl

S u e   H a m p t o n

The   Waterhouse   Girl

Pegasus

A CIP catalogue record for this title is
available from the British Library.

ISBN 978 190349 042 6

Pegasus is an imprint of
Pegasus Elliot MacKenzie Publishers Ltd.
www.pegasuspublishers.com

First Published in 2009

Pegasus
Sheraton House Castle Park
Cambridge England

Printed & Bound in Great Britain

This one is with thanks to all my loyal friends, in Folkestone, Capel Dewi, Hitchin, Watford and Berkhamsted, who had faith in me.

Chapter One

Have you ever seen a Waterhouse girl? They're in Tate Britain. And you might find one on an upmarket birthday card, the shiny kind. But right from the start I never really lived up to my name. My newborn head appeared sprouting tufts, like prairie grass after marauding herds have squashed it. And as I grew, my hair never did behave as well as the rest of me.

Eventually the name Daisy Waterhouse became what teachers call inappropriate. A bad joke. And that girl, that Waterhouse girl from the paintings all around me, became harder to be. As a story, it's not over, and there's no Cinderella ending, not yet. But it's a wild ride in its way, with whoops thrown in. I'm telling it for a few different reasons, and I think they're good ones. You'll work them out.

Looking back, I can see that on the outside, I was doing well. As if I was holding it together. I've always been more of a watcher and a thinker than a tantrum-thrower. It's in my diary that I find the purple words, the ones that cause a stir, like *broken-hearted* and *lonely* and ***freak***. There's an *I HATE KEVIN PRICE* in large black capitals, but it's crossed out rather furiously. I remember telling myself hating gets you nowhere. Nowhere anyone wants to be.

I was only a swan on the surface, head high. Underneath I was treading water trying to keep afloat, watching out in case anyone or anything tried to pull me under. More of a puppy, not used to deep water and waves, and barking madly, but not sure anyone can hear. Or a whale in shallows, beached and helpless, longing for the ocean.

Because what you see depends on how you look at it.

I'll start with an ending. There's a stripped and gutted house, and a day that changed everything. Summer. The start of the school holidays before Y6 began. Just the two of us, Mum and me, and a long wait for a removal van. Tension in the very empty air. And lots of pretending going on: words like 'coping' and 'for the best'. A day I never wanted to come.

It was my idea to leave the pictures till last. They were only prints, of course, and cheaply framed in clip-on plastic sheets, with dust creeping inside. And there were finger marks to be wiped from the surface because I'd touched the painted hair when I was small, thinking it would be softer than mine. We loved those pictures, both of us. Those Waterhouse girls with their waterfall tumbles of look-at-me hair had always been there, all my life. So, right up to the final hour they kept on smelling their roses, sailing off to die and opening up caskets to set evil free. Meanwhile all the rest lost itself in boxes all around them. Not that the wild-haired girls in the paintings were bothered about removal vans and boxes. They looked sad, of course, but even the bad things were beautiful in their world.

"Don't tell me you can't see they're sentimental! Should be on a box of chocolates, not a wall! Wipe your finger over and it'll come up sticky!"

That's what Dad told Mum, when the trouble started. He was grinning but his sentences weren't playful like they used to be. They were loaded and fired, and had a way of hitting their target that made Mum cry. If he had always hated the paintings, by a Victorian artist called Sir J.W. Waterhouse, he'd never said. He'd only joked that Mum had married him because he was a Waterhouse too. The pictures were one less thing to argue about. Now all our family still shared was the name.

Dad had already moved out, early one morning when I'd been too sleepy to cling to him and wail like I'd done in my dream.

"Bye, Daise," he'd said, as I stood there in my pyjamas.

He had taken the biggest case, the one I'd never been able to move an inch on holidays in spite of the wheels. It was surrounded by bulging plastic bags, even though I'd told him the house was a bag-free zone and hadn't he read about all those towns where people actually cared about the earth.

In the dream I'd begged and he'd put his arms around me, told me he loved me and stayed. The real life version had more silence and fewer smiles. I just nodded dumbly to whatever he said, which wasn't very much. We would still see plenty of each other. He promised, but it didn't sound solid. It sounded like a hope, a wish, a New Year resolution. I didn't want to count on it.

When I remembered the cold air in the doorway it felt a long time ago, but it had only been eight days. I hadn't seen him since.

"He'll be busy," said Mum, "but he'll be thinking of you."

Maybe he would. I imagined him in his white overalls with a paintbrush, flinging windows wide open, the cleanest painter and decorator in town, no trace of emulsion in his carefully combed hair or his neat fingernails. And I remembered the smell of him, before he started smoking again. He would be warm and glistening from the shower at the end of the day, almond and honey or coconut and vanilla trailing him around the house. When I was very small, my days had been over by then, and I'd cuddle up to the scent of him while he read to me from a picture book.

Mum hated him smoking. She had said if he loved her, he wouldn't do it. And it had turned out that he didn't love her, not enough, so he didn't stop and didn't care.

We were still sitting waiting for that removal van, ready too early with nothing to do and nowhere to be, when he phoned my mobile.

"Hiya, Daise. Whatcha doing?"

He talked like that sometimes, like someone from *Eastenders*, as if it made him cheeky and fun. I thought he should know it wasn't the right time to be cheeky and I wasn't in the mood for fun. It was what my head teacher would call 'inappropriate behaviour'.

I didn't say that what I was doing was crying a lot and how I was doing it was quietly.

"Tell him about your new campaign," Mum had said. That seemed inappropriate too but it mattered more than moving house so I did.

"I'm trying to save the polar bears," I told him. "The ice is melting and we have to reduce our carbon footprint so I'm walking to school even when it rains."

"Bet that was Mum's idea," he said. "She'll save money on petrol and lose weight at the same time."

"And we're not flying next summer," I announced.

"Drop in the ocean, Daise," he said. I knew it meant 'Why bother? One person makes no difference'. That made me mad.

"Sixty million drops would make an ocean," I said, and he laughed, so I put down the phone. And waited for him to call back, but he didn't.

Of course now our landline was disconnected and we'd have a new number along with a new address. Mum was trying to make it sound exciting: a fresh start.

"Couldn't you and Dad make a fresh start together?" I asked, while we sat on the window sill, looking out for the van.

Mum said it was too late and anyway … She didn't finish the sentence. The reasons the pair of them had given me for splitting up were like lines from a script that was so predictable the viewers could have written it.

And they sounded as if they had practised them and chosen what to tell but also what to hide. Mum said she couldn't talk about it any more, but she always changed her mind when she was in the kitchen with Auntie Sue. Sisters were allowed to know the things that daughters couldn't hear.

Mum kept the door almost shut, but the last time the two sisters got together round a table with red wine, she had let Auntie Sue call Dad a flirt who made eyes at women when he painted their hallways. I hadn't been listening exactly, but I'd heard, and I wasn't going to let it go.

"He's just sparkly!" I called from the bottom of the stairs, and the kitchen had gone so quiet I could hear the freezer hum.

14

The silence hung for a moment and Mum looked at me as if she was going to cry but I ran upstairs again before she could. I hated to hear them talk about him like that. And I was sure Mum used to love his bounce, his playfulness and impressions of puppies and crocodiles. Just like I had.

I used to wish I'd inherited more of it. I felt as if all the bounce I'd ever managed had slipped out of me, like a pump-up mattress with the stopper pulled out and the air escaping. But then I'd always been quiet, more like Mum. I had Mum's nose and Mum's hair, thick and wild and determined to tangle itself up again as soon as I put down the brush. Mum said I was a real Waterhouse girl like the ones in the paintings, but it wasn't really true. They had amazing, romantic hair that rippled and flowed and shone. It was beautiful, and not so much wild as free. Mine was a liability.

"It looks like a bird's nest!" Dad had said last Christmas. "One that's fallen out of the tree and been blown around by the wind."

The joke was not as funny as he thought it was, and Mum had told him so.

"It'll calm down as it matures," she told him. "Mine learned to behave. It's under control — most of the time."

Mum's hair suits her and the clothes she wears: autumn colours, mostly, but soft rather than bright. She's a painter too, but a different kind. Of course as we sat on the carpet waiting for that van, she didn't have a job any more, not yet, because she had been Dad's secretary, handling the phone calls and the money. But I knew she had talent. She can draw quickly and cleverly, even the really hard things like faces and hands, and her watercolours melt together like rainbows.

Her friend Liz owned an art shop in the town that was one stop away on the train and a half hour's ride away on the bus. She had been at Art College with Mum but I hadn't seen much of her since I was small because she'd lived in Scotland for years. It was where she'd grown up and I remembered that she spoke differently from all the other women I knew. And I had a memory of the sound of her: the jangle of jewellery and a deep but sucked-in laugh. Mum was going to work for her part-time and she said she was looking forward to it.

"Don't you think," I asked while we waited, "that you're wasting your potential?"

Mum laughed and said it was nice to know that someone thought she'd got some.

"Maybe one day soon Liz'll hang my paintings in the shop and I'll wrap them up and hand them over for a nice fat cheque."

The removal van really was late now, and the boxes were not very comfy seats. The carpet looked worn and shabby, and without the sofa we could see where the spag bol had landed when it flew right off the tray on my high chair. The house didn't feel like ours any more, and soon it wouldn't be.

"We'll be all right, darling," said Mum. "We've got each other. And our Waterhouse girls."

I could see the painting with the shipwreck where the girl watches the storm and can't do anything to stop it. The sky is grey, the waves are gathering into towers and the ship is going down. All she can do is stand and stare while the wind blows her fabulous hair. No one can see her face, but everyone knows she is crying inside and her eyes are wild with fear.

"If you look at it the right way," said Mum, "it's exciting. A new home and new friends."

There were lots of answers I could have given her, if the removal van hadn't drawn up on the drive. As it was, I tried a smile that felt crooked and let Mum kiss my forehead without saying any of them.

Then she pulled a face.

"Would you believe it! Now I need the loo! Last time, eh? They'll have to wait for us now."

She rushed off and I looked out of the window. But I wished I hadn't, because the removal men weren't the only ones out there. My dad was in his overalls, banging on the windscreen. I couldn't hear what he said because of the traffic but the men didn't want to know. They wound the windscreen up again and when he stepped forward to the cab they must have thought he might grab the handle because they pressed the button to lock him out.

I wanted to shout at him to go away before Mum came out of the bathroom and saw him. But she'd hear me. I was just about to open the window when he stood still and put both his hands on the top of his head. He held them there a moment, like you do with superglue while it sets. Then he ran off as if some thief was driving his van away.

Mum emerged and chatted to the men, and they must have kept quiet about my mad dad. The loading began. They were fast and strong and friendly. Mum and I just moved the lighter things into the hall once the big things made room for them. I went back to my room just in case something important that used to be under the bed got abandoned. But there was only a furry mint and an equally fluffed-up hair bobble that never would stay in place. My hair always sprang out like a jack from its box.

Oh no. NO. No, no, no. On the pavement below my bedroom window Dad was back. And he was lifting the coffee table from the back of the van, lugging it back down the ramp. I didn't know what he thought he was doing. But he had to stop. As soon as Bill or Aziz caught him they'd call 999. He'd be arrested or something. And as for Mum …

The mint stuck to my fingers and the hair bobble was so fluffy it would probably fly up and join the clouds, so I threw my mobile. I'm a good shot (goal attack) so I didn't hit his head. It landed beside him on the pavement and smashed into bits. Dad put down the table, looked at the Sim card and split red plastic and then up at me. I don't know what he saw in my face but I shook my head, pulling my lips together so that nothing came out.

"I'm sorry," he mouthed at me, and his hands went to his hips.

He breathed hard, as if he'd just finished a race. Then he gave me a smile. And he walked away, with a friendly wave and the same word mouthed again.

We left the house in the end, and the coffee table came with us, but the mobile wasn't well enough to travel. When I put it in the bin liner with the mint and bobble there were a few other last minute bits of rubbish lurking at the bottom. I pulled out a piece of sketching paper, thick and textured, and there was Dad again, drawn by Mum. I don't know when. He was smiling. Laughing, maybe. Happy. But not whole, because the picture had been torn, just once, not quite down the middle. I found the other half and put them both in my bag, the beaded, mirrored African one with tassels.

"Come on!" called Mum. "The lads are waiting."

That night I wrote in my diary. *Dad lost the plot.* That seemed to cover it.

I listed some cold facts about the flat, with its musty smell, its stock of art shop materials on the landing, the chipped worktop at the kitchen end of the small, square lounge and the toilet that didn't always flush.

I hate this flat. I hate what's happened.

Maybe I took a deep breath then. The rest is less angry and more thoughtful, but not any happier:

I didn't want to move. I didn't want to leave my friends, especially Jess. I'm not good at making new ones and I won't be able to sleep with the noise on the high street. I only pretend it's exciting because that's what Mum wants to do. I'm not excited. I wish I could rewind, go back to my high chair and the times they hugged and laughed.

Mum would say if we fast forwarded I would see there is happiness ahead. I don't think I'm old enough. I don't know how. And she only says those things for me. She's miserable underneath, and angry too, even angrier than I am.

I know I looked at the last part and wondered whether it was true, because I've never been the kind of person who loses my temper. But I decided there was more to anger than that, and that it doesn't even know, half the time, who or what it's angry with.

There were loud voices on the street below. Not anger, but laddish strut stuff. The music from the lounge was faint because Mum was trying not to wake me, but it was another of those heartbreak songs she kept playing, with violins mourning as if someone had died. Just picturing Mum's face listening to it made me forget about whether I was angry, because I loved her anyway.

I reached for my diary again but I couldn't write the words. I didn't dare. *Suppose I should have let Dad in? Suppose Mum would have forgiven him and called off the move and we'd all be home again now?*

I buried myself deeper under the duvet and imagined the Waterhouse girl smelling the rose, trying to fill the room with its scent. The paintings were still in black plastic but Mum had promised to hang that one in my bedroom because it was my favourite. It scores lower than the rest on tragedy.

Staring at the wall, I wondered whether there would still be room for a whale if Mum found time to paint one, life-size. Not a Blue Whale of course. That would be too big to fit along the Queen's bedroom wall in Buckingham Palace. But a Bottlenose might, if it was a baby. I decided to check, in the morning, and measure, once I'd found the pop-up book that had got me hooked when I was five or six. Not all the whales popped up any more, now that the card tabs had been pulled so many times.

Then I remembered something. I took the two halves of the torn portrait out from my bag and made them meet like the pieces of a puzzle. I laid them on the top of an unpacked box close enough to the bed for me to see Dad smiling. There was a gap in his grin where the paper had ripped, as if someone had knocked out a tooth with a left hook to the chin.

I sat my old teddy on another box and turned over. As I rolled away from him I felt the hair at the back of my head, wiry as ever. I patted it around the nape of my neck. It still felt thick enough. But when I brushed it a few minutes earlier, a lot had been left behind on the brush. I'd unwound every frizzy strand and wrapped it in tissue before I put it in the bin so that Mum didn't see. She had enough to worry about. So did I. I remembered something Dad said when my face looked serious and he thought I was being miserable: "It might never happen." And I told myself, looking at the hair still caught in the brush, that it might not.

"Night, Dad," I whispered to the wall and the boxes. "Sleep tight."

I could hear his reply: "If the burglars come, I'll put up a fight." Mum had told him off for that little joke because I used to have nightmares about those fights, and Dad losing them.

"I was only trying to think of something less creepy than bed bugs biting," he'd protested. Dad was frightened of minibeasts. But when I pictured him saying goodnight I could feel his hands tickling me like a hundred spiders.

All those memories seemed so long ago they might as well belong to someone else with a completely different life.

Mum appeared at the door, but I didn't stir. I didn't want another goodnight kiss, not if there was dampness left on Mum's cheek. Mum pulled the door so that there was a crack of light from the landing. I closed my eyes and shut it out.

Chapter Two

The days should have passed quickly. There was plenty to do, unpacking, settling in, finding our bearings in a new town. The Waterhouse girls still hid in black plastic, but that was because Mum was promising to decorate before she hung them. My bedroom wall wasn't completely bare, though, because the sketch of Dad, taped at the back, faced me when I lay in bed. I saw Mum look at it and away again. She didn't say anything, but she put her arm round me and I knew that meant the same as the word Dad mouthed on moving day.

The walls were odd colours, with grubby marks and a few spider leg cracks. I said I'd help, because I'd learned a few tips from Dad.

I'd measured up for the whale but Mum wasn't sure.

"It would be hard to capture the life and shine. You wouldn't want a great black blob, flat and dull and ugly."

Mum was not as good at life and shine as she used to be.

The shop below our new home was quite busy, considering it only sold fancy things like tapestry kits, multicolour feathers, sequins, goggle eyes and paper with grass in it. Mum said the people in this town must be very well off and have loads of time on their hands. I thought they must be very patient too, because so much of it seemed fiddly. In the flat we didn't have room for useless ornaments, just what Mum called "a survival kit".

At the end of Mum's first day at work, she did cry, because of the "stupid till". She said Liz was the loveliest, bubbliest boss in the world, who seemed really happy to have her there and kept hugging her. She explained the till with a few waves of her bangled arm and made it sound as simple as the two times table.

And after Mum had asked twice she couldn't ask again. So I had a look with her after the shop was shut.

I'm not that bright when it comes to technology, but I'm young and that makes a difference. I'm not scared of it; it's always been there. Jess is quick with ICT and always used to drag me behind, a bit like a three-legged race where the partners run at different speeds. I got to the tape in the end, but it was harder for me to help Jess with the things I was good at, because they didn't have step-by-step instructions. Anyway, I could help Mum make sense of the till, so she hugged me and cried again.

She kept apologising too. It was true that I'd known better school holidays. I couldn't even stay with Grandma and Grandad on Mum's side because they were on a cruise, and Dad's parents were younger so they still worked. I tried not to look or sound miserable, for Mum's sake. Even though that's what I was.

On the days that I hung around the shop, I was allowed to wander out on my own to buy something from the baker's or a takeaway hot chocolate from the café. But the best idea I came up with was the library, because time passed more quickly with a book in my hand. There were cushions where I could snuggle down and hope nobody noticed.

"If a librarian sees you there for hours on your own," panicked Mum, "she'll call Social Services and you'll get put into care."

Sometimes I had to tell my mum not to be so dramatic. She said things like, "You're doing so well, Daisy." I heard her telling Auntie Sue I was her rock, but I didn't even feel like a pebble. I wasn't really calm. It's called internalising and grown-ups don't want children to do it. I think I did it because it was easier. And less tiring. Or would have been, if only I could sleep.

When Mum had her lunch hour we would sit upstairs in the kitchen end of the flat, which had a bird's eye view of all the people coming and going along the High Street.

"She's a financial adviser," said Mum, if a woman wore a black trouser suit, carried a laptop and swivelled on pointy-toed shoes with heels.

"Here comes another Norman!" we said, if there was a man who was short and rather round, with glasses. That had been my idea. Sometimes we sang *Show Me The Way To Amarillo* because I said that was every Norman's favourite song.

"You wait, Daisy Waterhouse!" Mum told me. "One day you'll probably introduce me to a boy called Norman and tell me he wants to marry you."

"I'll only say yes," I said, "if he has kind eyes and lets me dance."

I didn't only mean dancing with feet, even though that was what I loved best. I meant dancing on the inside, where the ideas grew. I think Mum understood.

"That woman there," Mum said, looking down on someone pale and scruffy, with too much to carry, and a mouth set hard, "sings like an angel, but nobody gets to hear her voice any more, not even her."

I wondered whether that was what Dad meant by 'maudlin'. He had warned me not to let her get like that, but I could hardly throw away Damon Rice and David Grey. I couldn't stop her (once we got a TV) watching anything that had a break up, affair or death. That would leave *Countdown*, on a good day.

I looked down at the street hoping someone might be smiling.

"Some of these people are really happy, Mum," I told her. "They like their lives. It does happen."

But Mum was tired of the game. She put the kettle on.

If it was really sunny during the lunch hour we would go and eat a snack on the bench by the river. I'd try not to watch the time because I didn't want those lunches to end. I tried to pretend we had all day to feel the sun's warmth and watch the ducks.

"It's a pity Liz never had any children," Mum said one day, feeding the last bit of her sandwich to a duck. "She's mothering me and she's great at it."

I wondered whether I did any mothering for her and whether I was any good but I supposed I couldn't be.

"You can't paint that!" she cried, sidetracked by a hungry mallard, the colours on its head and the way they changed in the light as it turned. "Well, I can't, anyway."

"Too much life and shine?" I asked.

But Liz interested me, because she was colourful, with plenty of shine, full of words and energy. There was plenty of Liz too, but it didn't make her slow. Everything she did was fast and flickery. And she reminded me of a Masaai woman in Kenya with all her prints and home-made earrings that swung low. My favourites were shaped like constellations or animal footprints.

"Has she got a husband?"

"Liz? No!" Mum laughed. I couldn't see how my question could be funny.

"Partner?" I suggested. Jess's mum had one of those.

"She's an independent woman!" cried Mum, as if it was an achievement, a triumph. "Like we're going to be!"

"Can't I go and stay with Dad?" I asked, though I hadn't planned it and I knew it wasn't what she wanted to hear.

"He's busy with the new flat. It needs a lot of work."

"I could help."

"But I want you ... you need to get used to this new home before you have to cope with another. And besides, I'm having a week off soon, so we can explore the town properly. And go to London on the train."

I knew London was where Dad's flat was. Somewhere called Putney, which was too far away according to Mum. But she wasn't thinking of Dad, or if she was, she wasn't saying. She said she must book for the exhibition at the Academy.

"Cool," I said, smiling because that time I knew I'd said the right thing.

It was Thursday anyway and Dad was coming over on Saturday. Mum didn't talk about it. I'd heard them arguing on the phone about how long it would take him to drive over.

"Daisy would want you to get the train," Mum had told him, which was true. "She doesn't want to be ashamed of your carbon footprint."

Of course I hadn't heard Dad's reply to that, but I could guess.

"I'm not paying forty quid to wait on tube platforms." Or, if he was trying to avoid a fight, "Don't worry. Tell her I'll wear my coolest shoes."

My first visit to Dad's new home and Mum hadn't even written it on the calendar. But I couldn't wait.

That Friday turned out to be what Mum called 'significant'. It began when a girl my age came in to the shop with her glamorous mum. Liz greeted the mum, whose name was Kay, rather like a friend. I gathered she was a regular customer. As she talked, waving her arms, I stared at her fingernails, blood red and perfectly shaped. She looked more like an actress than an artist.

She told a long story about her neighbour "dropping dead". She was afraid the owners would be in a rush to find new tenants and let it to "somebody awful". I wondered whether her idea of awful people would be the same as mine (if I had one) or Dad's. In fact, I had an idea that on Dad's list, the awful people might include her. Along with Liz and Auntie Sue.

While the three women talked, the girl, whose name was Tamsin, stared at me as if I was something so rare David Attenborough had never seen anything like me.

Was it my grubby trainers, which had no logo at all? Or my freckles, which had been multiplying in the sunshine? I thought she looked at my chest as if I should have breasts. I noticed her bra straps, but she didn't need support. She was what Dad called a stick insect, a very small one.

"I've got a kitten. It's sooooooooooo cute!" she almost purred. "It's white as my teeth," she added, showing me how perfect they were, "and it has the prettiest little face. It's soooooooooooo gorgeous."

While she was talking she scrunched up her shoulders and clasped her hands together, a bit like a hamster with sunflower seeds. I remember wondering whether she really understood that her kitten was a living thing, a scratching, pooing, bird-chasing thing. Not an accessory. Tamsin had a lot of accessories. She held a pink and purple mobile and wore an ankle chain as well as a necklace with hearts on it and a matching bracelet.

Of course I thought it was probably my hair that made the biggest impression. Mum said when she was my age afro perms were cool, but she meant a kind of big fluffy seventies halo, not a cutting of thatch from a cottage roof.

Tamsin's hair was long and shiny and naturally blonde. I thought she should be on TV advertising shampoo. She looked as if she was wearing mascara and lip gloss and she told me she was a model.

"Oh," I said.

The mums seemed pleased to see us noticing each other, even though there was more staring than talking. Mine suggested that we went upstairs to play some music while Tamsin's mum chose what she wanted to buy. Kay seemed delighted and said she'd do the rest of her shopping too, and come back in forty-five minutes.

Tamsin looked around the flat as if it was a landfill site. She wanted to know where the television was.

"We haven't got one," I said. Dad had taken it because he cared about it more, and Mum knew he'd be lost without the football.

"You must have a computer?"

Tamsin lifted her sentences at the end like an American.

"Sorry," I said.

"It's a skanky flat," said Tamsin. I said I supposed it was.

"Got any good music?" asked Tamsin.

I shrugged and said it depended. I showed Tamsin the CDs but she wasn't impressed. In fact she summed them up in what Mum called a toilet word.

"I wouldn't come into your house and be rude about stuff," I told her, because I wouldn't. Even then I knew Tamsin's house wouldn't have a scummy bath and stained toilet. It would smell of potpourri and the sofa would probably be made of creamy white leather. The only thing that would be whiter would be the carpet. It would be so white that if the kitten sat on it no one would ever find her.

"We could spy on the people," I suggested, moving to the window, "and make up lives for them."

Tamsin stared as if I was very, very weird.

"Why?"

"It's fun."

Tamsin's face was full of pity and her eyebrows scrunched. Then I remembered that Liz had taught me how to draw Bart Simpson and Scooby Doo in a few strokes of the pencil the day before, so I showed Tamsin, who wanted to try herself and even muttered a quiet, almost swallowed, "Cool."

But she wasn't happy because hers weren't as good as mine.

"I've had more practice," I told her.

"I'm bored," said Tamsin.

I wasn't sure what to do about that. In the end I didn't have to do anything, because Tamsin decided to go shopping with her mum, who was in fact still talking downstairs.

"Have you girls been making friends?" asked Kay, stroking Tamsin's hair in a way that I thought was understandable but Tamsin didn't seem to like at all. "Daisy will be in your class next term, Tammy. That's nice, isn't it?"

"Mmm," said Tamsin, looking round the shop.

"Well, Molly," said Kay to Mum, "get in quickly if you want the house, and as I say, I reckon they'd sell if you made them an offer."

"I will. Thanks."

Then it was back to shop talk, stencils and lampshades and orders. While it went on I saw Tamsin, round the corner of the nearest aisle, reach for a pack of shiny beads. She saw me and smiled for the first time. And then I thought I saw her slip them into her little sequined clasp bag. I told myself I must be wrong. The rack still looked full. And it had happened in a blink. If it had happened at all. It must have been blinking that explained it. I'd just missed the moment when she put the pack back with the rest.

I looked at Mum, in case she'd seen something, but she was smiling. Tamsin was looking impatient now. She didn't turn or wave as they left, but I heard her join in the goodbyes, as if she was happy to leave.

After that there was a rush of excitement from Mum and Liz. Well, Liz told the story, most of it, like a trailer for a film, but no pauses, just plenty of hyped-up action. And because she needed her arms to tell it, the story rattled with bangles all the way through.

Apparently, thanks to the sudden death of Kay and Tamsin's neighbour, we had a chance of a proper house really quickly. Kay had said that she was sure she could swing it because the owner fancied her.

"She's the kind of woman who thinks that about all men," said Liz, with a little breath of air from her nose. "But it'll be a decent house even if it needs work."

"What do you think, Daise?"

I hadn't really forgotten the shiny beads. I thought of the orange wall on the landing and the handle on the toilet. I thought of Crystal the kitten, even though I really prefer birds. They're higher beings than people; flying gives them a kind of magic power.

"I don't mind," I said.

I knew Mum didn't like the flat much and that she would love a garden to care for. I said I loved gardens too, especially if I could plant more flowers if there weren't enough.

"It'd be great to have someone your own age next door, wouldn't it?" she asked me. She sounded so hopeful. I paused much too long.

"Maybe," I said.

Mum seemed disappointed, so disappointed that she might cry. She went to sort out some stock and Liz told me quietly in that soft Scottish accent of hers that I had burst my mum's bubble. She pulled at her purple ring as she said it, and then her green one. I didn't know Mum had any bubbles. I hadn't seen one for such a long time.

That night Dad rang, not long before he was due to come to take me to his place. Mum answered, and I knew from her face that something was wrong.

"You'd better tell her yourself," she told him, and passed the phone over. I thought the whole weekend was cancelled and it was my turn to have my bubble burst, a very large one. At that moment the weekend felt like the only bubble I had.

"Hiya, Twinkletoes," he said. "I can't come tonight after all. The flat's in chaos and I've got work in the morning. Couldn't turn it down. But I'll pick you up after lunch and we'll have the rest of the day, yeah? Do whatever you want."

"Okay," I said, trying not to give him a hard time because I could tell he felt bad even though he was working so hard to be chirpy. Mum gave me a hug and started to think about supper, since there would be no pizza after all. I wanted to say to her, *Don't. Don't say a word about him. Please.*

Just to make sure, I went to my room and read under the duvet. When Mum checked I was all right, I said, "Yes," without looking up from the book.

In the diary I wrote about meeting Tamsin, but not what she did. It might have been used as evidence. *We'll never be friends,* I wrote instead. *We'd both run out of words. And patience.*

Later, at bedtime, I had a shower and tried not to look at the silverfish swarming on the floor. I wished I hadn't told Dad about them on the phone the previous week because he'd made a big fuss and said Liz should get rid of them. I'd imagined Liz with a big net trying to catch them but they were so small they'd slither through the holes.

I washed my hair, using an old green plastic tube with a shower on the end that fitted on the tap, but it had a split that shot water out at ninety degrees. To save electricity, I didn't put the light on, but I could still see the silverfish wriggling around. They glisten, but not in a nice way.

It felt as if I still had a lot of hair, a whole thick mass of it, as I worked the shampoo through. But when I was out of the bath and trying to get through the tangles with a comb, a whole clump came away, like a tuft of grass pulled out of the earth. People talk about hair having roots, too. Liz had said that Kay needed to get hers done. But I thought mine didn't seem to be holding. I pictured my head, transparent like a glass vase, with roots dangling down inside, tickling behind my nose. But no hair on top. I imagined myself as a sci-fi robot with a shiny plastic head.

Of course the hair that had come away was only one tree in a forest. One floret of broccoli on a bunch. I had plenty more, more than anyone could possibly want. So no one needed to know, no one at all. I was getting better at secrets.

Chapter Three

I didn't complain that Dad arrived by car. I knew he would, and I'd decided he never listened. He was grumpy, though, about the traffic. Mum said public transport was probably quicker as well as greener and he asked whether her halo got stuck in doorways. But he didn't wait for an answer.

"Mum's not a saint," I told him as I clicked my seatbelt. "She's just doing her best for the environment."

"Can we leave the environment out of it?" he wanted to know, with a sigh.

I nearly said people had been doing that for much too long. But you can't campaign twenty-four seven. At least, I can't. And I was glad to talk about happy things. I wondered if he knew how glad I was to see him.

"The car smells of smoke," I said, as he drove off.

"All right, all right," he said. "I'll give up, I promise. I'll give up the fags and I'll sell the car and ride a bike in the rain."

"You won't," I said.

The car was a bit of a mess. There was a lump of old chewing gum wrapped thinly in tissue on the dashboard and I counted three empty water bottles knocking around on the floor. One slid under my seat and hit my ankle.

"Why didn't you just buy one and keep refilling it with tap water?" I nearly asked him, because Mum had been saying that soon plastic water bottles would be banned along with supermarket bags, so that they didn't make mountains on landfill sites.

"Give it a rest," was what he'd most probably say. He had said it before. Or "Give me a break."

I picked up the bottle and put it in the glove compartment without a word. Dad asked me to choose some music on the radio.

"I'd rather talk," I said.

"Talk away."

I was silent then. He laughed, but I thought he might not have done if he had known why. I didn't ask him what he thought he was playing at on moving day because I didn't want to know or remember. And there were too many things I couldn't risk telling him in case he snorted or blamed Mum for them. The toilet. The silverfish. The hair on the brush.

"That's your trouble, Daise," he said. "You'd talk the hind legs off a donkey."

"You talk," I said. "I'll listen."

"Ha!" he said, and added that he'd got himself into enough trouble that way. He put some old rock music on and tapped the steering wheel with the palm of his hand to the rhythm. He started singing loudly but I knew it didn't mean he was happy.

There was something I should have told him, even though he would probably blame Mum. And Liz. Even though it had been my idea, and I'd been thinking about it for ages, because it fitted.

"I'm vegetarian now," I said, trying to sound casual. He stopped singing and took a deep breath.

"Right."

I thought he would ask "Since when?" but he didn't. He just said it was a pity I hadn't mentioned it because he had bought a chicken.

"I can't set it free," he said. "It wouldn't get far."

"Dad!" I protested, and smiled, even though it wasn't as funny as he seemed to think.

He said we'd better go shopping for lentils and chickpeas and I asked him if he could afford a toothbrush and pyjamas and overnight things like that.

"So that they're always there, at your place," I said, "and I can't forget something important."

"And you can come any time," he added.

I nodded. I was excited again, in a nervous sort of way.

"Great," he said. "I'd better get used to toe poo. Whatever it is."

"Tofu!" I cried, and punched him, lightly and playfully, on the arm.

The drive back into London seemed to take for ever. I hated to see the jams, all the engines lining up and belching fumes. A bus cut across the little red Suzuki as if it didn't exist. Dad's face was tightening and he wasn't drumming rhythms any more. Then from nowhere a boy on a bike pedalled past on the inside as we waited at traffic lights. Just for a moment I saw his face, creamy brown and dark-eyed. On his back and front he wore a kind of runner's bib with a hand-painted L, thick and red. The bike was much bigger than he was, but his thin legs were long, like his hair. It splayed out under his helmet in a scooped up bundle of tight plaits.

His father was close behind him, a full-size version, same position over the handlebars, same focus. They looked intent, wary. I reckoned that was probably because they could get flattened like a jam sandwich any time.

"So irresponsible," said Dad. "Letting a kid your age ride a bike in London." He was trying to get a good look, and his face was quite angry. I didn't say that it was the drivers who were irresponsible, putting their own children at risk by destroying the planet. I thought they were cool, the thin boy and the dad at his shoulder.

I knew Dad didn't. He was following them ahead, threading through the queue to the lights. As they crossed the red there were noises: hoots and brakes and some kind of action we couldn't see.

"Think the rules don't apply to them! Look down from the moral high ground on the rest of us and then try to kill people!" Dad cried.

The moral high ground was a place he'd talked about before. He'd accused Mum of taking a stand on it. I wondered whether he thought I stood there with her, and whether I did. Or should. Because I knew it was about believing in things and I didn't know how it could be bad.

33

The boy and his dad were disappearing into the distance. No one lay dead on the road. Everything seemed normal to me as we moved on. Normal and tedious and thick with carbon emissions. I wanted to ask Dad why he hated cyclists, but he was still clenched, his hand tight on the gears. He'd never been an angry dad, not when I was small, but things had changed and I was worried he'd changed with them.

When we arrived at the new flat it wasn't at all what I'd expected. For a start it was old, but not in a good way. The street was busy and full of tall houses with gates, paths and steep doorsteps. Some of them had flower borders in front, or window boxes bright with colour. But 175 only had weeds, a tangle of them, sprouting out of two old pots and all around them. The wheelie bins sat in the middle of the jungle, full to the tipped-up lids.

Dad pressed a code as well as turning the key, heaved the door with his shoulder and stepped into a narrow hall where two bikes leaned against the wall, two helmets hanging by the straps from the handlebars. I didn't think of anything at first except Dad's road rage. I'm not the quickest on the uptake, and there were a lot of bikes in London. Then my mouth opened in recognition. It was them! Not only greener, but faster too!

Dad didn't seem to look. But he must know them. They were his neighbours. I felt excited now, but I didn't like to ask until he'd loosened up a bit. He was heading up the narrow stairs, which twisted round before another flight headed up again.

"You're at the top?" I asked.

"Yes," he said, "but not much of a view."

Once inside, I climbed onto the brand new, black fabric sofa and looked across the street to a roof garden opposite. The flat smelt of paint, but not the kind that made me sick. The walls were shiny but bare. There wasn't a lot of furniture but what there was all matched, part of a set, with more propped up in flat packs ready to be joined together. It looked too plain and new for a place like this, and the place itself was wrong for Dad. It needed huge wild plants and African hangings and Chinese vases. It needed different smells, and music.

Dad showed me the bathroom. It was brand new and shiny with paint. Better than ours, and greener too, as he pointed out smugly, because there was just a shower, no bath. Then he told me all the lights were eco ones that last for years.

"Are you proud of me?" he asked.

I told him no one likes a show off.

"Who are they, your neighbours on the bikes?" I asked, imagining a room full of all the patterns and colours Dad had left out.

"Bob Marley? The boy doesn't live there. The guy is on his own. Like me. We only have visitors."

"You should make friends," I told him. I had a feeling all his, apart from the plasterer and the electrician, were borrowed from Mum and married to hers. I wasn't sure he'd hang on to them.

"Hmm," said Dad, and started to check his fridge for things I could eat but it was full of beer and green cheese that made me want to throw up.

"I bet they've got tofu," I said. "Bob and ...?"

Dad didn't answer. He was too busy opening and closing cupboard doors and his mouth was turning down.

We had (yellow) cheese on toast in the end and Dad said not to tell Mum. I said it was great, even though the bread was the white kind that Mum said was a cross between chalk and plastic. Then he left all the dishes in the sink with a load of other pans and plates that must have been from supper the night before.

"Dad," I sighed, and soon had my elbows in bubbles. He dried. He didn't mind that part.

He wanted to know whether I fancied going to the fair. It was on Wimbledon Common, which was only a bus ride away. I wasn't a big fan of fairs, even then. They smell of fat and sugar and the thick black oil that greases machines. But I had the feeling that he had planned it, like the chicken, and I'd already spoiled that, so I just said, "Fine," and smiled.

The fairground was noisy as well as smelly. I had to shout at Dad even when I was right by his side. He was desperate to go on the rides, and asked one of the men which was the wildest. But after the candyfloss he'd insisted on buying, I said I'd probably throw up all over him. Then he took a pack of cigarettes out of his back pocket, looked at me as if he'd forgotten I was there, and put them away again.

"I know it was stupid to start again," he said, "but then doing stupid things has become a speciality of mine lately."

Like leaving us, I wondered? Or eating half a ton of bright pink sugar that looks like cloud but clings to the tongue like sand?

"Cheer up, Daisy," he said. "It's supposed to be fun."

But his eyes weren't sparkling, whatever Auntie Sue reckoned. I squeezed his arm and said I'd go on the Whirling Waltzer with him if he was really up for it.

"Promise to hold my hand if I'm scared?" he begged, like a wimpish little boy.

I couldn't help smiling and promised. It turned out to be such a nightmare that I've never been on anything like it since. But at the time, I pretended to be enjoying my terror, like some people really do. We were strapped into a car that didn't look too scary, and told to hang on tight by a boy who chewed more than he talked. It started off quite gently, but then it felt like a giant switch had been flicked and we were jerked and spun and juddered so that everything soft inside me wobbled and everything hard tensed so stiff it felt it could snap. Especially my neck.

I don't think I made any noise. Dad made enough for both of us. His mouth opened wide and what came out was long and loud and swelled up and down like a wave. I just hoped that nothing pinky-orange and lumpy came out with it, because I was feeling really sick myself. I just closed my eyes and let him hold on to me. But it wasn't over. In fact it had hardly started. The teenage boy was standing over a car full of screaming sixteen-year-old girls and spinning it just to make them scream even more. Then he moved away from them and towards us. Dad tried. He managed a word inside his noise and it was "NO!" but the gum-chewer was used to that word. It was just part of the game. We got the treatment. And I felt a bit like Anne Boleyn when the axe came down, except that she wasn't revolving faster than a CD at the time. I even thought it might be a relief to see my head roll away into straw. Because that would be the end.

When the real end came, I couldn't be sure my head was still on the top of my body, so I felt it. I stroked my neck. Dad and I held hands and didn't say very much for a while.

"You don't have to be nice and pretend you enjoyed that," he said, quietly.

"Did you?" I asked, because it was hard to be sure how he felt. He was always letting jokes get in the way, like decoys. I couldn't always see through them.

"FANTASTIC!" he roared, almost as loudly as that sound that had poured out for the whole of the ride, as if wherever it came from he had an endless supply.

His eyes were sparkling then. Even though they were red and his face was white. I didn't believe him, but I squeezed his hand as I told him he was a very bad liar.

"Thanks, Dad," I said, on the bus back to his flat. It was an old one, with a top deck, and we sat above the driver, looking down on his bald patch. That made me feel my own under the frizz. It was warm and a little bit damp. Now the top of my head would smell sweet like my fingers. I worried that if it was sticky too all kinds of things might attach themselves to it.

"You'd rather have gone to a gallery or museum," he said, sounding sad.

"No," I said. "Mum does that."

He still looked sad.

"Does she talk about me?"

I thought it was the hardest kind of question, the sort with wrong answers that will cause a real upset. Only it's hard to know which answers they are.

"It's all right," he said. "Don't answer that. I'm being stupid again."

"She misses you," I told him, in a rush, no planning.

"How do you know?" he asked. It came straight back, like a ball, hard and fast, when I hadn't expected it to be returned at all.

"Because I do," I said, but it lifted like a question. I was sounding like Tamsin already.

Back at 175 the weeds were under attack. At the front of the house, behind the bins, the boy was caught up in bindweed spiralling like barbed wire.

"Good idea," said Dad.

"It'll go in the compost," said the boy. "It's not like it'll die. Exactly."

"It'll help new stuff grow," I told him.

Dad seemed in a hurry but it looked as if he had forgotten his code. The boy was wrapping himself in the vine on purpose now, and grinning. I smiled back.

"Daise, when's your birthday?" Dad called, agitated.

I called it out, day, and month, but he wanted the year too. Didn't he know? It wasn't as if he was a Victorian papa with thirteen different birthdates to remember.

"Okay, broadcast it to the street, why don't you!"

He told me he'd chosen it because he wouldn't forget. I didn't say so, but it might have been better, I thought, if he'd memorised the date Tottenham won the Cup. He'd never forget that.

"Hey! You're two years, two months and two days younger than me," said the boy.

"That means it's your thirteenth birthday tomorrow," I calculated. His grin was wide. Dad was waiting by the open door so I said, "Cool," as well as "Bye."

As we turned to climb the second flight, the door on the landing opened and Bob Marley stood there in an apron with a fruit bowl on it.

"Cézanne," I said, because Mum's taught me. I know paintings, even when they're round people's waists with creases and sauce stains.

He seemed impressed, and reached out a hand to shake mine. It smelt spicy. The aroma through the doorway was enough to make anyone hungry, candyfloss or no candyfloss.

"Hey," he said to Dad.

"All right?"

"I got a load of food here. Sweet potato curry with cashews and banana. I wondered maybe you wanna help us out."

I liked his face. He reminded me of a poet Mum fancied. His feet were bare and brown and he had a hooped earring in one ear.

"That's very kind," began Dad, in a voice I recognised because of the *but* that was coming next. It came. "But we're sorted really."

What I wanted to say was "Dad!" but I didn't want to hurt him, so I just said, "Thanks, Bob," as they went on up the stairs, just as Bob said, "Another time."

Once inside the flat Dad asked me why I had called him that.

"What? Bob? That's his name."

"No, it's not. It's what I call him, after the singer who died. He might think you were taking the ..." He hesitated. I knew the word he didn't say because Mum didn't like it. "Bob Marley was the Rasta guy. God of Reggae," he went on instead. He shook his head at my ignorance. "You young people know NOTHING!"

So he put on a CD and showed me how to dance to the slow beat.

"Exactomundo!" he told me. "You got rhythm, girl!"

He hasn't. But I liked it. I had liked the boy too, and the sound of sweet potato curry. There was a knock at the door, and there he was, when I opened it. There was a still a short trail of bindweed around his calf.

"Hey," he said. "Are you really sorted?"

I looked round at Dad, willing him to admit that sorted was the last thing he was or felt.

"Yes, thanks," he said, sounding tired. "We're fine."

"Okay," said the boy, "but come for birthday cake tomorrow, yeah?"

"Thanks," I said, and watched him run barefoot down the stairs, his hair beating lightly on his back. I closed the door and hoped Dad wasn't going to reach for the breadbin.

"We'll get a pizza," he said, clapping his hands, and started to press keys on his mobile. I remember thinking that football facts weren't the only numbers he knew better than my date of birth.

Later, as we sat on the rug and ate out of the boxes, Dad asked me if he had done the wrong thing. I didn't know what he meant until he nodded towards the slice that was threatening to drip a string of cheese on its way to his mouth.

"I wanted you to myself," he said.

"It's okay," I told him. I could still smell the banana curry.

"But you like the boy."

"Yes, but I like you too," I said, and left out the *sometimes*.

That Sunday morning we listened to *The Archers*. He didn't tease me too much when I asked him to put it on, because he knew Mum always listened. There was an affair going on and Mum was very caught up in it. She had cried about it the previous Sunday. Tamsin, who would think anyone who listened to *The Archers* was very, very weird, had asked me which one of my parents was having the affair. I hadn't answered because it was such a rude question. And so stupid. I had talked about whales instead because that's something I can always do.

After singing along to the closing theme together we walked into Putney in thin sunshine. We went all along the bridge, looking over into the water just in case.

"Liz said they see dolphins in the Thames these days," I told him. "Porpoises too."

"And there are fairies on the banks," he said. "Look! One just landed on that coke can."

I glared at him.

"I'm serious," I said, and he said I always was.

So was the shopping trip. He bought toiletries, a hairbrush, slippers like sharks' jaws with soft white padded fangs, pyjamas with constellations on them and food that I called "proper". I checked the ingredients for animal fat and additives and stopped him buying cleaning products without eco-friendly labels. Someone had to. He was clueless in those days and I told him so. I made him pay out for a giant canvas holdall when he was trying to bag everything in plastic. I picked a card with a dolphin on that said HAPPY BIRTHDAY. It took a long time to choose and Dad seemed relieved when I finally dropped it in the trolley.

"They didn't have one with a fairy on a coke can," I said.

On the way back to the bridge we passed a shop selling mobiles and without a word, Dad dragged me in by the arm and began a long, boring conversation about networks and contracts which had a very happy ending: a small red mobile in my hand.

"Text me any time," he said, "and I'll text back. Only I might have to put down my paintbrush first, and come down the ladder."

"Thanks, Dad!" I cried.

"Don't throw it at any strange men," he added, his mouth curling.

"I only know one," I said.

When we stopped again on the bridge, there were people rowing below, but no sign of any large mammals. I sent my first text, to Mum, which read: *Dad is getting sorted. See you later. XXX.*

Back at the flat I slipped the dolphin card under the door and then worried that he wouldn't find it. I wished I knew his name.

I helped Dad make a salad for lunch. As he looked over my shoulder at all the red and green slices on the chopping board, he tried to pat my hair playfully.

"We didn't need pan scourers on the list," he laughed, as his hand came down.

I dodged like a dog afraid of being beaten and made for the fridge.

"You're not funny," I said, "and I don't like you touching my hair."

I looked back at his fingers, just in case they were gummed up with hairs, like the bindweed round the boy. There was nothing there.

"Sorry," he said, and tried to hug me. I let him, just for a moment, but I didn't want him near my head. There had been more on my pillow and in the new hairbrush. Which meant less on my scalp.

I hadn't expected to miss Mum, but by the afternoon, when Dad put the cricket on, I was missing her a lot, and wondering how she was managing without me. So I was glad when the boy knocked again.

"I brought you cake," he said, holding out a plateful. "Carrot and passion fruit. Dad made it."

It looked amazing, and as I thanked him I hoped Dad was listening.

"But tea is off. Uh, cancelled. Sorry."

"Oh."

"Thanks for the card, Daisy."

"You're welcome," I said, hoping he would offer his name.

"And sorry again. Got to rescue Mum, see."

Dad had moved closer, perhaps to the cake, I thought.

"Anything we can do? She's all right, is she?" he asked.

"Oh yeah," said the boy. "She's been arrested again."

He almost smiled. I realised that Dad had no idea what to say, and wasn't sure I could do much better. I didn't know any prisoners then.

"I'm sorry to hear that," I said. "It must be a case of mistaken identity."

"Nah," the boy said, hands in pockets now. "She's guilty. Always is."

He turned to go.

"See you soon. Enjoy the cake. We're taking some to Mum."

"That's nice for her," said Dad, in a tone Mum wouldn't have liked. I called out "Good luck!" as the boy ran away. At the turn below he stopped and called back.

"My name's Flame. Like a dragon. But I don't bite and I can't fly."

"See you, Flame," I said, and shut the door.

I admit it now. I thought he was the single most exciting person I had ever met in my life. My diary says so. This time I didn't write it because I was boiling over. I wrote it because I liked my life a lot better now that he just might be in it. Even though I had an idea, from Dad's silence, body language and general storminess, that he had a different point of view.

Chapter Four

Sometimes life picks up and becomes full of action, like an episode of a drama that everyone talks about. I thought, as Dad drove me home, that weekends were never going to be the same again, that Flame and I were going to be friends and he was going to show me some kind of exotic new world. But I didn't tell Mum about Flame or not-Bob. I was saving them up until there was more to tell. Besides, she didn't want to know too much about my weekend. She was just glad to have me back.

Then everything took a different turn. We were moving again, much sooner than anyone would have expected, because there was no chain.

I was pleased. Just not that pleased. Mum could tell, but it was hard to explain why. I hardly knew Tamsin. I hadn't chosen her, not like Jess and I chose each other, slowly, in a growing sort of way. And as my diary says, more than once, I wanted Jess. Not Tamsin at all. I wasn't sure about her being quite so close, every day, in and out of school. It didn't matter, though, what I wanted. I was going to step into a new world, but it wasn't Flame's, and it wasn't full of banana curries, or wildly heroic mothers behind bars for breaking laws that must be unjust. It was Tamsin's world, and it was full, as far as I could see, of make-up and shoes. And not much else.

Mum and I visited them, and the house that would be ours, long before we moved in. Liz came too, to measure up for curtains which she would sew when things were quiet in the shop. It was a dull house then, but the toilet flushed. Tamsin said she wouldn't be able to sleep in it, because the old man had died there.

We were in her house, which was nearly as white as I'd predicted. Mum and Liz were next door, busy imagining and sharing ideas of how it could be transformed, brought to life after the tiredness and the death.

"He might be a ghost," Tamsin said, stroking Crystal the kitten under her small, trapped chin. "How creepy is that?"

I said it wasn't creepy at all.

"He can carry his head into my room any time he likes. I'll call you if he does and you can introduce us."

"You're weird," she said.

I'd only known her a couple of weeks and she had called me this about thirteen times. It was true: she brought out the weirdness in me and made me proud of it. I heard myself saying things just to make her pull one of her incredulous, creased and open-mouthed faces. Sometimes in my mind I told Flame about our conversations and imagined him laughing.

If you're wondering what happened about Flame, I just had to wait. I went to Dad's the next weekend, but they weren't there, either of them. And the weekend after that I went with Mum to see Grandma and Grandad, who were back from the cruise and lending us money for a mortgage. They were kind, of course, but rather a hushed, poor-you kindness. I told Mum it made me feel like a Victorian flower girl but she had to outdo me and say they treated her like a cholera victim in a workhouse.

Meanwhile the school holidays were being eaten up. Jess still wasn't back from Australia and the summer was like a whirly seaside ice cream with only a melty blob dripping from the cone.

So I didn't want to spend what was left of it with Kay and Tamsin, but they invited us. Well, Kay did, and Mum was too polite to snub them. They showed us round the town, the parts we hadn't discovered yet, including the castle. It's in ruins, but that's more exciting in a way. I told Tamsin I could imagine it the way it used to be. I tried to turn my mind into a computer, take the crumbled leftovers and build on them until I could smell the past as well as hear it. Even though I agreed with her that the thought of a poor old pig turning on a spit was really gross.

"Listen," I said, "and you might be able to hear the clatter of armour and the creak of the drawbridge lowering across the moat."

I rattled on about jousts and dungeons, but she interrupted and her mum told her not to be rude. I could tell Kay liked me. Mum said she thought I was clever and I knew Mum didn't think Tamsin had much "going on upstairs". That was what she'd told Auntie Sue in the kitchen a few nights before.

"I want an ice cream," said Tamsin again.

Kay said no at first, but not for long. Two minutes after Tamsin stormed off in a hip-swaying sulk we were sitting on the grass eating cornets with flakes balanced in amongst the swirls. The mums were talking carpets. Tamsin, who was staring at my bruised bare legs, asked me where I got my shorts.

"The Oxfam shop, I think."

If Tamsin had known what her face looked like, she wouldn't have made it. Her mouth lifted closer to her nose and her eyes came down to meet it. She looked short-sighted.

"Sad," she muttered.

Kay took a breath and chipped in.

"Tamsin won't wear anything that hasn't got the right label."

Mum and I laughed afterwards wondering whether she meant one that said £2.99.

It was the start, in a way, of project makeover. That was what Tamsin wanted to give me. I didn't realise then, even after the ice cream drama, that she never gave up on anything once she'd decided she must have it. I told her I'd rather explore in the woods but she didn't want to do that, even though she had the best bike with a million gears. But then I found a distraction, the only thing we both enjoyed: dancing. Of course we didn't like the same music, but I copied her moves and she copied mine.

"You're quite a good dancer," she'd told me one wet afternoon.

I'd made something up to a track she liked, and closed my eyes so I wouldn't see her face as she watched. I knew she meant it, because her voice was quiet, and not quite glad.

"Thanks," I said.

"Weird, but kind of … good."

I smiled. Not 'cool', of course. I was certain by then that Tamsin would never, ever use that word about me.

She showed me all her medals for ballet and tap and modern, on the pale pink walls of her bedroom. I thought of coconut ice every time I stepped inside. I think she sprayed it with sweetness: vanilla, strawberry. And everything wasn't just tidy, but arranged.

I did a quick detective scan for anything made of tiny beads but there was nothing. Why would Tamsin steal something that cost three pounds when she had everything she wanted? It made no sense and I told myself I'd got it badly wrong.

She was producing her big fabric-covered Chinese box rattling with expensive make-up.

"I'd soooooo love to make you over."

She was doing the cute little girly look that worked with her mum when sulking didn't. I was getting fed up. This was probably the ninth time she'd asked.

So this time I said she could make me look like Pocahontas if she liked.

"Or a white tiger," I added.

"Derrr!" she said, scrunching up ugly again. "It's not face painting. We're not five."

She told me how much the make-up cost as if I was supposed to be impressed. I wasn't. It was enough to feed a family in Africa for a month.

"Makeovers make people look better," she said, slowly, as if I was five after all. "Foxier. Hot."

We had different vocabularies. I was beginning to think we came from different planets.

"You could look so much nicer," she said, making the word sound soft. "Oh go on, Daisy. Please. I'll make you look sooooooooo pretty, I swear."

I supposed it was a compliment: she thought that was possible. It was the kindest thing she'd said to me, and I was tempted. I did wonder whether all the girls in my new class were going to be like Tamsin. I looked at her pleading face. She was desperate to do it. It seemed mean to spoil her fun if she wanted it that much.

So I said yes. I didn't worry, exactly. I just hoped that I wouldn't end up like the human-sized doll's head on her shelf, because that had more eye liner than Cleopatra.

She sat me down on her white wooden chair with the padded pink seat, in front of her enormous mirror, at something like a desk that wasn't for writing on. All around the walls on either side of it were photographs of Tamsin, made over for modelling assignments.

"I'll never look like you," I said, "whatever you do."

"No," she said. "Not many people can. But you're interesting. Mum says. "

That pleased me because I decided I'd rather be interesting than foxy. But looking at Tamsin, preparing for her task like a surgeon lining up scalpels, I knew I'd have to be mad not to want to swap hair, since hers was completely perfect and mine was compost. I knew she was pretty and I wasn't. But I didn't hate my freckles, even though she looked at them as if they were some kind of contagious outbreak. Or warts. And I knew, even then, that my look was different. Probably because I was weird, of course. But that didn't matter, because it was mine, much more than her look was hers.

I thought she'd begin with make-up, but she took a big pink brush and started somewhere else. On my hair. Straight in. No warning. Just a rough, determined tug. It was as if she knew it was going to be like tackling the garden of the dead man's house: more of a battle through untamed wilderness than a glide over a carpet-smooth lawn. I made a small protest noise that asked her to take it easy. I tried not to panic but it didn't work. So I tried to stop her with words, offering to do it, asking her to leave it. She didn't take any notice and just lifted the brush out of reach when I tried to grab it.

I didn't pray because I'd stopped doing that the day Dad left. I didn't cry. I let go and stayed calm the way grown-ups always want you to do. I hoped for the best, like I'd done when Mum and Dad were arguing. And it made me feel brave and strong, as if there was nothing she could do to hurt me, as if I was dancing again and good at it.

So for all of three of four seconds I sat there, telling myself the bald bit was probably smaller than it felt. And that since there was so much hair, and it would never behave for anyone, she'd give up before she found anything.

"Oh my *God*, Daisy!"

Even then I told myself she meant undergrowth, effort, tangles. Dandruff, even. I knew a few snowy flakes of that would be enough to shock her into a horrified squeal. But when I looked in the mirror I saw she'd frozen, like a figure turned to stone in a fairy tale, like a teen star in a horror film. I could see her open mouth in the mirror, and her blue eyes were almost afraid. I didn't move, not a muscle, but inside everything stretched wide around an enormous NO. Because I knew the rumour was the truth and the smoke meant fire. And I waited, for the details after the headline, because she was the reporter on the scene, the one who could tell me the facts I ought to know.

Everything really did slow and soften, blur and tighten at the same time. Just like it did when Dad said, "Daisy, your mum and I have got something to talk to you about." It was only the second time that I'd been at the core of everything instead of the edges, and melting but solid. Hot but ice, and heavy. Too heavy for the space I filled.

I suppose I could have written her lines because I'd known, really, just like I'd known before the big, *let's all sit down* announcement. They were words, but they broke through sucked-in air, in a kind of high-pitched whisper.

"You're bald at the back, underneath your hair. There's a great big patch of BALD skin."

She started to investigate busily, pushing clumps of bushy frizz aside in search of patches of hairless flesh. I don't know about the skin on my scalp, but on my cheeks it was pricking with rushed-in heat. I saw the redness, saw my eyes brighten damp at the edges.

Apparently there were two small ones the size of pound coins, and another big one just behind my right ear which was "Massive!"

"I'll show you," she said, and looked for a hand mirror, the kind hairdressers give you so you can see how neat the back is. Offering to be helpful. And that was it: the lever, the ejector seat. A different NO. She couldn't make me look.

So I ran downstairs and slipped out of the front door while she called after me.

I had to knock at the house next door, the one that wasn't ours yet. Liz answered, with Mum behind. I must have looked in quite a state because I didn't need to say a word. Mum just held me while I shook. I didn't cry. But it hurt more than crying. I felt the heat of me soak into her as she held me and my breathing raced before it slowed again.

Mum didn't say a word either, not at first. Liz disappeared and left the two of us there, in a hallway that didn't belong to anyone, with a dead man's duck head umbrella handle sticking out of a tall jar by the door.

Her mobile went. I saw KAY but she turned it off. She just waited for me to stop shaking. It took a while. Then she pulled back to look at me, to read my face.

"Tamsin?" she asked.

I nodded, though it wasn't her fault. She was just the detective at the scene of the crime, not the murderer.

Mum kissed the top of my head, where the hair was rough but thick. She had no idea, of course, and she must have wondered why I started to sob. So I lifted up the hair and left her to look, because obviously it wasn't hard to find.

"Darling," she said, and for a moment I thought she was going to cry too. But she didn't. She smoothed down the hair and hugged me again while she talked over my shoulder. She spoke quietly at first, but the speech got firmer and louder as it went on. It began with something she'd never told me. She'd had alopecia herself, when she was about fourteen, and then again, after I was born.

"Alopecia?" I repeated. I hadn't heard the word.

"There are different kinds. This kind, like mine, is areata. Patches. The hair grows back, like mine did."

Then she said doctors thought it might be caused by stress. Or, in the case of an Olympic swimmer, falling out of a tree.

"You haven't been falling from trees and forgetting to mention it?" she checked, and we both made a noise something like a laugh, but in my case not so different from a sob either. I shook my head.

So then she said it was her fault, hers and Dad's, and she was sorry. Of course I couldn't let her take the blame. If I could have lied convincingly about a fall, I might have remembered something: a wall, a bump on the head, a collision with a hockey stick. But I'm hopeless at lies, even white ones.

"Maybe I just need vitamins," I suggested. Mum said there were supplements we could buy, so I nodded again.

"It really doesn't show," she told me. "You have to hunt for it."

"I know," I said. "It's a jungle up there."

Mum gave me a smile that meant she thought it was brave of me to try to be funny. It was something I got from Dad now and then and I hoped she appreciated that.

"Let's go," she said. "I can't make you hot chocolate here."

She wanted to know if I liked the house. I said yes. She wanted to know how I felt about living next door to Tamsin, and I remembered the brave me, who decided it wasn't her fault she wasn't like me, and that she was probably really sorry now that she understood how much she'd upset me. I could have said I never wanted to see her again, because it would have been true. But I weighed the house and garden up against the silverfish and toilet, the drunks on the high street on Friday nights and the traffic at all hours. And Mum's bubble.

"Tamsin is okay," I said.

I remembered Tamsin's words, the exact words and the way she said them and the face she wore. I didn't quote her. After all, she'd had a shock. She hadn't had time to think how she would feel if she was the one with a bald patch under her beautiful blonde, perfectly cut, pop star hair. So she hadn't worked it out that if she was me she would be lying under the duvet refusing to get up ever again. Sending away food on trays. Shouting "Leave me alone!" Wasting away with only MTV for company and surfacing only far enough to click the remote.

So I suppose in a strange way, Tamsin made me feel strong. Mum and I went for a walk by the river. We didn't talk very much but we linked arms, even though I had been through a phase when I'd felt too old for that. I didn't ask about the other kinds of alopecia, even though I could guess what one of them was and what it would mean. We just enjoyed the sunshine.

Back at the flat Liz asked me to try out a stained glass kit so she could display what I did in the window as a kind of ad. I concentrated hard and she said it was fantastic. She hung it straight away. I guessed that one of the calls she took on the desk was from Kay, because she was using words like, "Fine", and "No worries", and said how brilliant my stained glass was. Girls fall out. Everyone knows that. Except that I don't. I never have. Jess and I have never upset each other once and we never will.

Even though Mum can't always read my mind, and that's sometimes a good thing, she must have known I was missing Jess. She told me over supper that she would ring to invite her to stay as soon as we moved into the house. The bed at the flat only just fitted into my room and anyone sleeping on the floor would be a) bent like a banana, b) trodden on every time either of us went to the door, and c) concussed if that door moved.

I would have rung her but she was still away. So I sent her friendship vibrations and felt hers zinging back.

As I sat reading on the sofa after supper that night I wasn't expecting visitors. And certainly not the smoky one who burst in as if he'd run all the way and had to rush off again any minute. If alopecia was caused by stress, I decided Dad should be losing hair by the handful.

My heart sank at the thought of Mum calling him about my alopecia aereata because it made it a big deal, a drama. I wished she hadn't because I wanted to forget all about it and just act as if nothing was happening until the hair came back. So I looked at Mum after he'd hugged me in a sorry sort of way and she knew what I was thinking.

"Your dad needs to know when you're upset, love," she said.

"I'm not," I said. "I was over it. I was fine."

"Can I see, Daise?"

I stared at him. I couldn't believe he'd asked me that and I wanted to say "NO". But Mum had seen and I didn't want him to think he came second because that was what he thought already. So I lifted up the hair and listened for a gasp.

"Nothing to lose sleep over," he said, after he'd had long enough to think of it. "Or hair."

I ignored that, picked up the CD he'd brought for me and slotted it in. I turned the volume high. They went in the hall. I pictured them standing by the stock boxes, whispering. I'd never felt so angry with them before. I had to force my feet at first, but they kicked to life the way they always do, when there's a rhythm. I danced, with my eyes shut, and sang along with as many of the words as I knew.

Soon, Mum asked whether I wanted a hot chocolate before Dad went. She looked calm. Perhaps she'd told Dad off in her quiet, *I'm the adult* way that she uses sometimes when she's not upset herself. I danced over to the door to look at Dad in the hall. He looked the same as when he'd arrived: on edge. No, guilty! That was it. Same as Mum. They were sharing the guilt, not dishing the blame. They'd decided they had done this to me together.

For just a drumbeat I imagined a solution they might have found, but I told myself I knew better. My parents would *not* get back together to make my hair grow. And I knew they shouldn't have to do something they didn't want, not for me. It wouldn't work. They'd be unhappy. And I'd be the guilty one.

I had stopped dancing. Dad saw me watching as he checked his watch.

"See you, Dad," I said.

"Not if I see you first," he said, and attempted a grin with a mouth so straight it was more like a letterbox than a smile.

"It's only hair," I said. Mum was in the room now, looking at me too. "It's not blood. I'm okay. I'm fine. I'm used to it now. It's nothing."

They both tried smiles then, and Mum's was an improvement. I thought maybe I'd convinced her. Dad left, and she didn't cry quietly in the bath.

53

I wrote in my diary that the whole day was like a snowball that had been rolled around so much it had become a boulder and flattened people. I knew Mum and Dad loved me, and I knew they were trying to help. But what I wanted they couldn't give me now. Because sometimes the things you worry about shrivel up and blow away when you talk about them with your parents. But sometimes things end up scarier when adults get hold of them, take them away from you and talk them through as if they're not yours any more and they're scared too.

I'm frightened, says the diary. *I don't want to be and it's silly but I am. And I was okay with it before, when it was mine.*

What I wanted was my secret back.

Chapter Five

I tried to get ready for my new school. I don't just mean the list: pencil case, ruler, rubber and so on, or even new shoes, although Mum said I must be having a growth spurt because I needed those too. I tried to prepare inside, and talk myself out of worrying. But nobody gave me a chance.

It wasn't Jess's fault her parents decided to move to Sydney. The Australia trip had been a try-out, an investigation, and the result was that her dad accepted the offer of a job. The family would be back, but only for a couple of weeks, because everything was already set up. Jess hadn't told me, but then Jess hadn't known.

When her mum drove her over to visit, the day before term started, I felt awkward in a way I never had before, not with Jess. We were still in the flat, but only just, with boxes packed all over again. The two of us sat on the window sill looking down on the high street, talking about what was happening down there rather than upstairs, on my head, or in her future.

"Do you want to go?" I asked, in the end.

"Yes," she said. Her hair was bleached and her skin was browner. "Apart from you."

"We can email," I said, "once we've got a computer."

I think she knew I wasn't happy, but she'd known that for a while. I nearly told her about the alopecia, and how Dad had taken me to a dermatologist who prescribed an oily lotion that made my scalp a) feel like it was frying and b) smell like a farmyard. Instead I let her tell me about Australia and made her promise to send me a photo of her with a koala bear.

I didn't mention that the lotion wasn't working and neither were the vitamins and minerals. I'd lost a lot more hair since the makeover and if the wind blew the back of my head I could feel the coldness of the air on my scalp so I knew the curtain of hair had been pulled. No hiding place. There was no wind in the flat, obviously, so I don't think she saw anything. But I should have told her. Mum was hoping I would, and I meant to. Only I remembered the wide-smiled face she wore when she sat in the front row and watched me dance in the summer concert. If I showed her my head I'd have a different face to remember when she'd gone.

"You're still my best friend," she said, when she left.

"We'll be back in a couple of years," said her mum. I suppose that isn't much when you're old, but it didn't seem like nothing to me.

I remembered Dad with his giant case on the doorstep and the words that were so light they blew away like balloons.

Then Jess cried and that started me off. Our mums said encouraging things and mine cried too.

"You've got other friends," Mum told me, once they had gone, and I didn't argue. But a best friend is something different, and besides, there were a few miles between me and the others now. Neither of us used the word Tamsin, although she had tried hard to be nice to me since the makeover, so nice that she'd been persuaded to go on a picnic in the woods and lend me her bike. Kay hoped we'd be in the same class, and I said, "Mmm," but I didn't really know whether that would be such a good thing.

I could have said, "I've got Flame," but it wouldn't have been true. At least, not then.

That night when I went to bed, I told Mum the scalp lotion made my head itch so she said to leave it for a couple of days. My uniform was hanging up on the door handle, all ready. A baseball cap sat on my chest of drawers but that was for emergency use only. Dad had bought it at the weekend, and made a big thing of how cool it was.

"I'm all right about school," I told Mum, because I could tell she was worrying for me.

But in my diary I wrote:

I'm dreading school because I'm much too different now – I'm not just an oddball but a FREAK.

It's all on its own on a page, in large pink letters and the last word in rather artistic capitals. I remember the pen, with its strawberry scent, and when I read that word again now I smell it. And remember hating myself for using it. So I pulled myself together, and on the next page there's a list of reasons not to be afraid at all:

1. *I get on with other kids.*
2. *I get on with teachers.*
3. *I can do the work.*
4. *I like learning (as long as I don't feel pressured or babied).*

So when I closed my eyes I planned to get a good night's sleep and wake up brave.

I slept, give or take a few strange dreams about flesh-burning dragons and my head being beaten around by a rounders bat and rolling in the dust. I was just stirring around seven when Mum came in to see if I was awake. I rolled over and we both saw it on the pillow: not the usual pattern of hairs, thin as a finger trail wiping the steam from a window, but a glut. The end of a ball of wool. A mess, still warm.

She picked it up as if it was alive and sleeping and she didn't want to hurt or disturb it. Of course we both knew there was enough hair to make a difference but neither of us was in a rush to find out where it was from. But I felt the top of my head. Lucky guess. Spot on. Mum saw too, as I sat up and looked in the mirror. There was hair on both sides of the pinkness, but was it enough to arrange, to spread thinly, like watered down jam, just enough to cover the cake?

Mum tried. I stood there watching. We both knew it was no good, not now. We looked at the cap and Mum sat it on my head, very carefully. Longish bits hung down over my ears and at the back of my neck, so no one would have known what wasn't underneath.

"It suits you," said Mum.

It might have done with jeans and trainers, but with the uniform it looked odd. Only neither of us admitted it. Mum wrote a letter to the head about me wearing the cap in class, but even while she wrote it I was wondering what would stop someone pulling it off. Apart from super glue. As she folded the letter and slipped it in an envelope Mum started talking about wigs, and said she'd ask Liz to let her look up suppliers on the internet. She said ladies who lose their hair can get them from the hospital, on the NHS, but they'd be too big and too grannyish for me. She started chattering on about companies that make wonderful wigs for Jane Austen adaptations on the BBC but I couldn't see that ringlets would be much use for Harford Junior.

"Will you be okay, darling?" she asked on the doorstep when I was all ready in my shiny new shoes.

"Course," I said. "Just a bad hair day. Everybody has them."

I reminded her that there were children in hospital with no hair because they were very ill, and I was fine. That seemed to make her weepy although she didn't want me to know.

Kay was picking me up and taking me to school with Tamsin because it was a bit too far to walk. Suddenly Mum said we could go on foot after all, if I preferred, as long as we legged it. I was telling her again that I'd be all right when something fell through the letterbox just as I was about to open the door. It was a card, with a whale on it, and inside it said:

Have a good day at your new school. See you at the weekend.

Flame

I grinned and put it on the window sill in my bedroom. Of course Mum wanted to know who he was. Anyone would have thought he'd asked me to marry him, the way she was probing.

"He's a boy with great hair," I said, "and a cool bike."

When I told her about Dad's neighbour she said, "Ah," and didn't ask any more. But as I got into Tamsin's car, and she stared at my cap, I thought of him. And as we drove away, with Mum waving, I took it off, and slipped it in my school bag. It was a warm day. I didn't want to sweat. And I imagined Flame smiling at me.

When we arrived at the school I saw how big it was: not just the building and grounds but the crowds of pupils everywhere, swarming like the silverfish. Tamsin seemed in a hurry to be out of the car. I followed, trying to catch up with her. She was waving to a group of girls in the playground.

I didn't expect her to introduce me. She acted as if I was some sort of shadow behind her, but certainly not hers. If she was ignoring me, though, the other girls didn't quite manage. They didn't say anything, but their eyes did. They connected with each other and back at me. As if I was the point of the triangle. Isosceles. The smallest angle of the three.

"I'm Daisy," I said, as brightly as I could, "but I'm a bit short of petals at the moment."

I imagined Flame laughing. It was a Dad sort of joke and he would have been proud of me. Tamsin wasn't, and the only girl who laughed actually snorted.

"Neighbour," said Tamsin. "Are we going in or what?"

I kept my distance behind her as she talked with her friends, but had to follow because I didn't know where to go or what to do. Tamsin didn't tell me. I just did what she did, and ended up in a large colourful classroom with 6Y on the door. A teacher with very short, shiny hair spotted me straight away and said I'd come to the right place because I was in her class. She looked like a ballet dancer, with a long neck and beautiful hands, but her neck and eyes were older than her walk.

Or her name. She told me she was Mrs Young.

"Do you know anyone already, Daisy?" she asked, showing me a drawer with my name on.

"I know Tamsin," I said.

Tamsin heard, and looked up as if she had been shot. I sat down next to her like Mrs Young suggested. She didn't speak to me, but when a boy sat down on the other side of her she told him something funny I couldn't hear and he laughed.

Mrs Young told everyone who I was and asked them all to help me settle in quickly. She sounded as if she was sure they would be really friendly. I didn't trust them like she did. So I painted Flame, in my mind, smiling at me across the room.

The lessons were fine. Mrs Young didn't just look musical, she had a voice like a character in a stage show. It sounded as if any minute it might lift just enough to begin a song. And her hands were like birds, taking off, soaring, hitching a ride on a thermal. I used my hands too, to answer questions, and ask a couple too. Tamsin soon turned her shoulder and angled her elbow away from me but I pretended not to notice how wide the space between us had become.

At playtime I decided I was too proud to hang around Tamsin unless she wanted me to, so I gave her the chance to invite me, to smile or just to make the kind of eye contact that means it's okay to be there. She acted as if she'd forgotten I existed, and disappeared with a couple of the girls she'd met before school. I looked around the emptying classroom for someone who might look at me but everyone was heading outside without noticing I was there. So I took my book outside with me, found a corner and read it standing up, leaning against a wall. No one bothered me at all until a group of boys running past me suddenly stopped and backtracked. They had a long look and ran off in the midst of some noises that weren't quite laughter, but if there were words there I couldn't make them out.

Thanks to some real words on the page, time went quickly. I'd had months of practice at concentrating on my reading when things were happening around me. Then maths went quickly too, because I enjoyed solving the problem Mrs Young set, the kind where you find your own way in. But lunchtime was an hour, and I couldn't take my book into the dining room.

I knew that if I told Mum everyone was talking about me, she'd say I was being oversensitive and imagining it. It didn't feel like my imagination. I ended up sitting next to a girl called Nina who didn't speak much English. I felt sorry for her and smiled a lot but she didn't understand anything I said. After I'd eaten my dinner I hung around in the playground, wandering, as if I was exploring. I found a spot on the church clock across the field and stared at that. I did look for Tamsin, but she was in a huddle of girls with teen magazines. They turned their backs on me as if I might crane my neck to find out which celeb had dumped who and whose summer legs had cellulite. I imagined Flame at secondary school, surrounded by girls just wanting to smile at him.

Back at the wall, looking at the clock, I had a visitor. It was a very blond boy called Kevin who was in my class. Mrs Young had had to move him to the front of the carpet. He was walking over to me as if he had a reason, and some of the other boys were watching. Looking. Waiting.

His fist reached out to me, knuckles up, but not like a boxer. More like the game where you have to tap the hand that you think is hiding something. But he wasn't waiting for me to choose. His other hand was near enough to grab my arm and hold me still if I didn't play. And I wasn't going to run. I think I knew he had something for me, and my brain was telling me it could be anything but sometimes there's a place inside, near where you breathe, that knows better. It had tightened and I was having trouble being the swan because the puppy thought it was drowning.

He handed me something, pressing it into my hand without speaking, swallowing a laugh. Even before I opened my fingers I recognised the firm, packed centre, the yellow disc. It felt warm and squashy, and that solid core was breaking into tiny specks. And that was how I felt, as if it might as well have been me. As I looked at it, the laughter broke too. A daisy with all its petals plucked. Then as the tightness hardened my memory worked it loose. The power of getting there first. My idea, not his.

Kevin was laughing loudest and I wondered what would happen to his face if I said it. So I did.

"You stole my joke."

I said it so quietly I only just heard it myself. I don't think all the boys did, but Kevin heard, and I got my answer. His skin set, no creases, no looseness round an open mouth. Tight like pastry when there's no more stretch however hard you roll.

"I what? I stole your what?" he cried, volume up. And I wished I'd just cried. He would have been happy then. It would have been over.

"Who stole your hair then? Was it the fairies?" He had an idea. I saw it cross his face. "Was it a farmer? Did he need a new scarecrow?" He grinned. "You could apply. You'd scare away the crows. Just stand there. Like that."

One of his friends nudged him because the lunchtime assistant was eyeing the group of them and heading towards us. They were gone, in one move, one wave crashing onto the steps into the other playground. I blew out secretly, reminding myself how you breathe without the tightness inside.

The dead daisy was still in my hand. I dropped it over the fence into the overgrown churchyard and looked for Tamsin. She was right at the opposite end with her back towards me, but she looked round, bored, and I smiled just in case. She waved, mouth wide, and I waved straight back. But then a tall, good-looking boy brushed past me, focused on her. As he loped towards her and her smile cooled to teen queen, I turned away and looked back up to the clock. You're okay, you're okay, I told myself. Unhurt. All right. Keep breathing.

In the afternoon we had a dance lesson in the hall. At the word 'partners' I resisted any urge to look in Tamsin's direction. But Mrs Young needed someone to demonstrate with her. Maybe Mum had said dance was what I do best. In any case, she picked me and seemed really pleased with me, even though all I had to do was balance her body shape symmetrically. When it turned out there was an odd number of children because someone had to leave for the optician, she asked if I would work with her.

I smiled and wondered what Tamsin would think of me dancing with the teacher on my first day, especially as our piece was way better than anyone else's. Mrs Young didn't just look like a dancer, she moved like one, and I loved it. Every twist. Every curl. Every reach and hold. The audience watched in something like amazement. Maybe they were waiting for me to tread on Mrs Young's toes, or fall over, because I had a feeling their mouths were itching to laugh. But I didn't, so they couldn't. And at the end a lot of people clapped. It felt respectful, and very surprised.

I didn't check Kevin. And I didn't care whether the applause was actually all for Mrs Young. I was warm anyway, but it was a different kind of heat, softer. It didn't squash, like my hand on the daisy. It filtered through the space and made room for me to stand and feel it.

"You've got real grace, Daisy," she said, just to me. "I'm going to have to keep an eye on you."

I smiled, but I knew there were things she wouldn't see and I didn't want to show her.

At the end of my first day at school Tamsin didn't wait for me, like I had assumed she would, so when I looked up in the cloakroom and found she'd gone I hurried outside in case Kay forgot me too. I could tell when I saw the car and climbed in that Kay had been telling Tamsin off for abandoning me because she was looking out of the window with a hard glare and a small mouth. Had I had a good day, wondered Kay. Had I made new friends? I made *Yes* do for everything and she soon gave up.

But back at her house Tamsin was her home self, not exactly chatty, more interested in the telly than me, but normal. She asked me to do what I'd done with Mrs Young so we re-enacted the dance.

"It's not hard," she said then, as if the clapping had been over the top.

I did wonder whether I'd done something at school to annoy or embarrass her, but if I had, I thought maybe she'd decided to let it go. By the time we danced together she seemed to like me as much as she liked most people. I supposed then that I knew what I'd done, and I hadn't meant to. I hadn't pulled the hairs out just to make it hard for her to be seen with me. I did try out a *sorry* in my head but I saw Flame shaking his head firmly. So I was just extra nice instead.

Of course Mum was harder to dodge than someone else's mother, and back at the flat, over supper, she asked the kind of questions it's hard to wriggle away from. I didn't lie. I left out the daisy with the petals torn off and Kevin's face, but there were things she guessed anyway.

"Some people aren't very big and strong when it comes to what people think. I'm sure Tamsin didn't mean to let you down. Image counts a lot for her. We all know that!"

The two of us smiled.

"But you are. You're incredibly strong. Strong enough for two!"

I supposed I didn't care as much as Tamsin about what anybody thought of me, the way I looked, being cool, fitting in. And I remember thinking that did make me strong. So I flexed my muscles in a stupid, Dad way. I didn't feel tough, not in my stomach. But I knew Mum believed it. She believed in me.

And then I remembered that a few children had spoken to me, like when I asked a girl called Megan where we put our outdoor shoes and she'd shown me, just like she would have shown anyone else. And when I'd asked another girl what time afternoon lessons started, she'd told me, "One fifteen, I think." They hadn't all acted as if I was invisible. And the head had asked me how I was getting on and seemed friendly. I told Mum about the lessons and of course especially the dance. I told her Mrs Young was lovely and described her hair and clothes and reported everything she'd said to me. But we both knew you can't have a teacher for a best friend.

"Tomorrow will be easier," I told Mum, before she could tell me. Dad said the same on the phone.

"First day's always hardest. Piece of cake from now on."

That made me think of Flame and the best cake I'd ever tasted. I practised what I'd tell him: a different version, including the joke Kevin had stolen. And I thought he'd be proud of me. He'd think I'd done the right thing, like his mum when she got arrested. But I wasn't as sure as I thought he'd be. The word 'provocation' came into my head. Mum used to throw it at Dad when he was driving and honked his horn in protest. Asking for trouble. After all, I'd got trouble already.

"You gave Flame my address," I told Dad. "He said he'd see me at the weekend."

"Okay," said Dad, "if that's what you want. I'll speak to Kyle."

So I knew not-Bob's real name now. But Dad's voice told me that I didn't know much about this boy. He didn't sound very keen, or glad, or interested. Afterwards I thought maybe what I heard in his voice was worry. I wasn't sure why.

"Yes," I said, because what I wanted to do was see Flame, "it is."

"Okay," he said again, and told me he was sure I'd get used to my school really quickly now. "And they'll get used to you."

I didn't know whether it was one of his jokes, his *being slightly rude about me* jokes. Or whether he meant the way I look now. The hair. Or not-hair.

"I suppose they'll have to," I said, strong enough for two.

"Someone's got to put up with you," he added.

And I nearly said something about people putting up with him too, except that Mum and I didn't, not any more, not day in and day out. No one did. I wondered whether he was lonely, because clients aren't the same as family, however many cups of tea they make, even if there are biscuits to dunk and they smile a lot.

I told Mum my first day could have been a lot worse and she hugged me. I didn't tell her how hard it was to look forward to the next one, or the one after that. When I shut my eyes I was more afraid than my brain wanted me to be. I saw Kevin's face, looking at mine. In my diary I raged about a *wicked* boy, but then I changed the adjective in case anyone thought I was using it as a way of saying cool or great, and it became *mean*, underlined five times as if I knew the word just didn't do the job. *And Tamsin,* I added, *doesn't know what the word friend means.* By the time I fell asleep my pillow was warm and damp and in my dreams I lost so much hair I couldn't breathe because I was choking on it.

And then Flame was cutting off plaited lengths and attaching PVA to my scalp until we looked like twins.

"Bro!" I called him, and we slapped palms, smacking loud.

"Sista!" he cried, and we smiled in the mirror together.

It was one of my better dreams.

Chapter Six

Kevin Price left me alone, more or less, for the rest of the week. Unless you count looks and wheezy, spluttery mutters, and he wasn't the only one entertaining himself with those. It crossed my mind that he might be plotting something. I should have known. But I told myself that whatever it was I'd cope. Grown-ups have to do a lot of that. I'd heard Mum tell Auntie Sue she was doing it. Coping.

Mrs Young gave Mum the name of a dance class run by a friend of hers, and when we found out it wasn't the one Tamsin went to, Mum signed me up. I got plenty of smiley faces on my work and scored three goals in basketball.

"See?" said Mum. "They'll forget you haven't got as much hair as Tamsin. They're used to you already. You'll be getting party invitations soon."

So I was coping all right until Friday lunchtime. I was hanging around with Nina, the girl from Poland, managing to communicate with mime and pointing when she didn't understand. I saw Kevin. And co: the others who attached themselves if he let them.

"Hey, it's The Turnip!" he cried.

Laughter. There's a phrase about your heart sinking and it felt right, because I'd been treading water trying to keep afloat and his voice turned something inside me solid and heavy and hard. I saw a boy called Yaz ask what a turnip was. He was overweight and I suspected he wasn't getting his five portions a day of fruit and veg.

"Turrr ni-ip!" chanted Kevin, like a football supporter waving a scarf, then stopped while the others echoed. "Are you stuck, like in the story? Do you need us to pull?"

"Hard!" yelled Yaz.

Hard, I repeated in my head. *I know that's what you think you are.* I thought it, but I didn't say it. I couldn't. All I managed to do was tell him with my eyes, just for a second, before I had to look away.

"How hard are you, Turnip?" he wanted to know, and smiled as he thought it through. "Turnips get mashed."

I didn't want to look scared. I needed him to think I didn't care. But it was the way he said the word. Mrs Young had mentioned onomatopoeia and even though Kevin wasn't the sort of boy who seemed to pay much attention, he'd got the idea, because he mashed the sound itself into a soft, spreading pulp. I was frightened. I couldn't help it. It was my head he was talking about and my eyes couldn't out-fix his, not any more. They were starting to burn.

There was only one thing I could manage and my feet did it. I walked away and the boys didn't follow. Someone must have said something witty because there was loud laughter behind me but I just walked on.

I thought it might spread. I didn't guess how quickly. Along the corridor I heard some Year Ones say it at the sight of me returning to my classroom. In the cloakroom at the end of the day I heard it again. Turnip. Apparently more than one Year Six boy was having it for dinner. The government would have been pleased at the sudden popularity of a tasty root vegetable full of vitamins. Turnip. At the school gate someone called it, high and clear: "Bye, Turnip! Have good weekend."

It was Nina. She didn't understand.

"You too!" I called, and ran for Kay's car.

By half past eleven on the Saturday I was at Dad's flat. I'd lost more hair the night before but I'd left the cap at home and he wanted to know why.

"Why not?" I asked. I felt excited, but nervous.

Dad wanted me to have lunch with him first, just the two of us. Then we were all going for a walk along the river, Kyle and Flame and Dad and I. Dad said it was going to rain, but I didn't care. I thought the drops might feel funny on my almost bare head.

"You can touch," I told Flame, as we walked past the rowing club. "I don't mind."

"It feels cold," he said, when he'd run his hand over the surface.

"I'm okay," I said.

Dad and Kyle were talking behind us but they must have seen so I smiled at Dad to tell him I was cool, not chilly.

"Why did your mum get arrested?" I asked. "Is she in prison now?"

"Daisy!" protested Dad, as if I'd got no manners, but I knew Flame wouldn't mind any more than I minded his hand on my scalp.

Kyle answered. His ex-wife had been protesting at the London Arms Fair. She didn't agree with selling weapons to anyone, including governments. There had been thousands of people demonstrating and some of them had been arrested. In her case, she had used a bicycle lock to chain herself to a gate.

"They covered it on *The News*," said Flame.

"We haven't got a TV," I said.

"Cool!" said Flame, and I gave him the biggest smile, because I didn't know anyone else who'd say that. No one. And I felt proud, which made a change from weird.

"Dad couldn't survive for a day without TV," I said, and Kyle asked, "Really, man?"

I could tell Dad felt a bit sheepish, but I looked at him as if to say I'd only told the truth. He seemed shocked when Kyle said he didn't care too much for football these days.

"Too much big business, y'know? Fat cats. Dirty money. Making out it's life and death when we got the real thing."

He said he liked it on the beach when he was a boy.

"Where was that?" asked Dad. "The Caribbean? White sand and blue sea?"

"Scarborough," said Kyle, and laughed a quick, sharp laugh, as if a pocket of air was caught on his tongue, but not for long. He kept smiling long after the breeze had blown it away.

"Dad's accent is all over the place," said Kyle.

"Well," said Kyle, "that's where I've been. But not any more. If the bike can't take us, or the train, then we stay put."

I knew Dad would be fed up and heard him change the subject, but I wanted to move ahead of the men and talk to Flame properly. I scuttled off a bit and hoped he'd follow. He overtook, and picked up a pebble to throw in the Thames. He could do that skimming thing, where the stone leaps like a deer across the water and out of sight. I loved it. He did it again, and talked me through, showing me how to hold it. Mine went plop. A bit like a turnip really.

"What's your mum like?" I asked, after we had run again, and waited on a bit of wall.

"A bit mental," he said, and chuckled. "Paler than you. Fair hair in a fluffy pony tail. I've got a half-brother who's really blond. But I'm like Dad."

I told him I knew that. I said he was the spit and he laughed as if he'd never heard the phrase before. He decided to try a big spit into the water but Kyle told him not to be such a dirty yob. I didn't think Flame could be a dirty yob if he tried. But told him I knew someone who could, someone in training.

I had to talk quietly, but I told him the story. Kevin and The Turnip. It was only Episode One, of course, but I didn't know that then. We were dodging behind trees, hugging them while we were about it, so it was in instalments.

"You're doing great," he said. "He knows you're not for mashing. He can't touch you because you're WAY bigger than him. You're out of his league. You're a giant. If you're a turnip, he's a pea."

It wasn't real, this picture of me. I'd left out the fear and the sickness inside. But I felt myself turn pink with the happiness of it, of his faith in me. I laughed so loudly Dad grinned at me, but looked left out. I wasn't going to share the joke. He wouldn't get it. He'd be down at the school demanding to see the head. He wouldn't believe I was a giant like Flame did. He'd just want to pierce the pea with a very sharp fork.

"You could make turnip spread," said Flame, "and take it in for packed lunch. Offer it around. Steal his joke."

I wasn't sure. I thought Kevin Price would hate anyone who stole his jokes. I knew I wouldn't like to be hated and I wasn't sure he hadn't started already.

"You're the coolest girl I've ever met," said Flame.

"Thanks!" I said.

I wasn't sure Dad thought Kyle was quite so cool. They looked strange together: Dad with his leather jacket and jeans, but some rather smooth shoes gleaming out like pointed snouts but getting muddy, and Kyle with his rainbow-coloured tapestry-style jacket ballooning out in the breeze over red and black swirl baggy trousers and purply red Doc Martens. Dad's hair was looking very sharp and I'd already teased him about it. Kyle had enough hair for twenty regular dads; I guessed it outweighed his boots.

Maybe Flame and I looked odd together too, but that was the point. We were both different, equally different in our own ways. I'd been picking up petals left behind from summer and held a handful of them: ox-eye daisies, big and cheerful. I was about to make a joke when I saw that Flame, a few paces ahead of me now, was looking intently into the water, his lips apart.

He beckoned. I stepped forward quietly. I saw a movement, a curve of bending water. A power push. Something big. The water, which had seemed clearer with sun shining on it a few weeks earlier, barely glinted now, dingy brown and cold. I couldn't see what it might hide.

"What?" I whispered.

His hand did a leap, a curling down somersault. I mouthed the word: Dolphin?

He nodded without taking his eyes from the dark surface. The wind was tugging at it now, but below the force was stronger. It was around the middle of the river, where the water was deepest, so it was quite some distance away from us. The dads had seen us watching and stood at our shoulders now. The river was a short drop below, edged by reeds clogged with litter, the plastic bags flapping like giant, old used hankies. Kyle's instinct was to lean down and clear up but Flame stopped him with a hand.

Trust Dad to spoil it. Full volume Funny Man.

"Not more mermaids!" he said. "River's overrun with them these days. We need a congestion charge, a tail-free zone."

To be fair it probably wasn't him who caused the problem, because a rowing eight was starting to thrash towards us, all grunts and shouts and big male bodies heaving away with their oars. It was enough to scare a Great White Shark. I didn't see what happened down below. Whatever it was, it must have gone somewhere.

Flame didn't give up until the crew tore straight across the centre of the river, leaving a pattern like a feathered arrow to trail behind it. Even then he followed the spot in front of the boat with his eyes, in case the dolphin was there, diving ahead of it. When the rowers had gone and their shouts faded he looked crestfallen for a moment before the excitement brightened him again.

"Dolphin or porpoise," he said. "I couldn't see the nose, just the way it moved underwater."

He sounded like a wildlife cameraman. I believed him completely.

"It's very early," said Kyle. "Most sightings have been January to April."

"Cold enough for January," said Dad, shivering.

"Shall we call the BBC?" I asked.

"They wouldn't take it seriously," said Kyle.

"Because we're kids," said Flame. He didn't sound resentful. "Anyway, we don't want a news team around. Point is, it'll be back. We gotta be vigilant."

I liked the way he said the word. It sounded so important. But there was a problem.

"We'll be at school," I said.

"Do I have to, Dad? Can't I keep watch with a camera? It's education! Real life kind."

Kyle grinned, but said it was a nice try. So at that point Flame wanted to go back to his dad's flat and get their bikes to chase after whatever it was and locate it, wherever it had gone. I didn't know how to feel. I had no bike. If they went, they'd go without me.

And they did. Flame was kind; he knew I'd be disappointed, but what he said was, "You understand, Daisy." I smiled. Of course I did. "We got a sense of porpoise now!" he added.

I gave him a huge smile even though his joke was bad enough for Dad and part of me wanted to cry.

"Text me," I said.

"Got no mobile," he said, "but I'll see you soon. Next weekend, yeah?"

I helped Dad cook tofu. We watched a DVD he thought I'd like, but I didn't care that much. Then on the Sunday we had a surprise visitor with a bag of scissors and combs and sprays. Her name was Sharon and when she walked in she brought with her an invisible cloud of flowerless scent. It smelt more like medicine but it actually made me cough.

She kissed Dad on both cheeks and he kissed her back.

"You must be Daisy," she said, and looked straight at the top of my head where the straggly bits were still hanging on. "I've come to neaten you up." She looked at Dad. "Not too much to work with," she said, in a lower voice, "but we'll have a go."

She was quite young. I could tell that from her clothes and shoes as well as her round, pretty face. Her skirt was short, and her tights black down to very high-heeled, two-tone shoes. Her own hair was spiky and streaked and her mouth was dark red, like a plum.

I gave Dad a glance that told him he might have warned me. He looked a bit awkward and put the kettle on. Sharon sat me on a chair with a tea towel over my shoulders, even though she said we didn't really need one, did we, and smiled. She started snipping. I was waiting for her to point out that it wouldn't take long.

"Your dad says you're clever, Daisy," she told me, "and very good at dancing."

That's the kind of comment that's rather difficult to answer. I gave her a kind of smile instead.

"He's worried about you, darlin', but I told him it'll soon grow back as long as *you* don't worry your head about it."

I wondered which part of me should worry: my right foot? I also wondered why she called me darling when I'd never met her in my life.

"So take no notice of people and they'll think you're making a fashion statement, eh?"

Maybe she was being kind but I didn't like the way she spoke to me as if I was six. I didn't know why but I didn't like the way she spoke to Dad either. Then I realised: Sharon was the explanation for his funky new haircut.

Mine didn't take long and when she'd finished she showed me in her hand mirror. All she'd done was make all the hair that was left the same length: short, but not dangly any more. It was an improvement and I thanked her.

"Less like an accident," said Dad, "and more like a plan."

Sharon's laugh was high and wobbly, like her heels. It lasted a long time. She drank her tea and I left them to it while I lay on my bed with my book, expecting her to leave as soon as her mug was empty. But nearly an hour later I emerged to investigate and they were on the sofa, so close I wondered whether she'd been giving him another trim.

Dad looked awkward again and she said she must go. I wouldn't have thought too much more about her if it hadn't been for Dad's question:

"Do you like her, Daise?" and a second, following it up because I didn't answer straight away. "She's fun, isn't she?"

"She's okay," I said.

There was a pause. Then he wanted to know what I'd like to do and I said I'd like to go home, please. I thought he'd argue, but he didn't. We didn't talk much in the car because I had an idea there was something else Dad wasn't telling me.

I didn't mention it to Mum: Dad's got a girlfriend. I had no proof, just like Flame had no proof he'd seen a dolphin (or a porpoise) in the Thames. I think, though, that I was nearly as sure as he was, and I might find out a lot sooner.

My diary for that night wasn't miserable. It concentrated on Flame, and the things I did know. It read:

Flame – the facts so far:
1. *He loves living things.*
2. *He thinks it's okay to break laws if they're wrong.*
3. *He's an ace cyclist and a fast walker.*
4. *He's mad about peanut butter.*
5. *He smells like a wood after rain.*
6. *He doesn't stare at my head. He looks at my eyes and ME.*

I wondered whether he was a good dancer, pictured him moving to the reggae Dad had played and smiled. He was bound to be.

Chapter Seven

Mum had arranged something while I was in London. I was already signed up for a dance class, but now Mum was going to learn too. It was something to look forward to, she said, and after all I never went to Dad's till the end of Saturday morning so nine thirty would work out fine.

I was pleased. I thanked her. I said I loved dancing better than anything else. But she knew I wasn't as happy as she'd hoped I'd be, and I didn't want to use the word "Sharon" or the word "school" because then her happiness quotient would drop like one of those vertical rides that just plummet while everyone screams.

But there was a whole week of school before the dance class and I felt quite sick on the Monday morning. When I told Mum she just looked sorry for me but she didn't even bother to feel my forehead. She knew I wasn't ill. She hugged me, told me how brave I was being and promised me I'd make friends soon.

Tamsin was quite cheerful on the way to school because she'd had her ears pierced and wanted to tell me how much it hurt and how easily the little red holes could get infected. She said when the time came to take her sleepers out she'd have to lie down or she'd probably faint. I thought afterwards that Tamsin would never jump out of an aeroplane or crawl down a pothole so this was the closest she'd come to being a hero. I smiled and listened to her detailed descriptions of the kind of earrings she would choose from (if she survived the removal of the studs without being admitted to A and E.) I'm good at listening.

Of course once we arrived at school she spun away from me as if we were magnets repelling each other. I said hullo to

Nina who looked worried. She sat reading quietly in the classroom, pointing to words as if she might learn them by concentrating hard enough. I was at the end of the register, being a W. When Mrs Young reached me, Kevin slipped in an extra couple of words that caused a little murmur of amusement. I knew what they were. It was my name now.

Some of the others were reading too, and one of the books was a picture book, a familiar one. Kevin was passing it round, pointing to a picture in it. The Enormous Turnip. Mrs Young probably didn't understand why any Y6 boy would be reading it, or what was so funny. How could she?

"You should tell," said Tamsin at break time. "They're stupid."

"It's just a nickname," I said, "like Teapot or Doughnut."

"I'd tell," said Tamsin.

She wasn't in a good mood any more because she said her friends were jealous of her pierced ears and accused her of showing off. I'd noticed that Tamsin's friends were the on/off kind, the tell-on-you kind. Like her. But I could see that she was trying to be nice to me.

"I don't want to get anyone into trouble," I said this time.

Especially as it would mean trouble for just about the whole school. But the real reason wasn't so big. I wanted someone to like me, and I was afraid nobody would if I whinged and snitched. And I wanted Mum to be right about me, so I thought if I practised not caring it would toughen me up until I really didn't care any more. After all, Kevin could have thought of a much meaner nickname if he'd tried hard enough, and once this one got too old to make anyone laugh, perhaps he'd try.

But by then I'd be as brave as Mum thought I was.

I did wonder about the other kids, and whether I would join in the way they all did, if the girl with the turnip head was someone else and not me. Would I whisper and stare and giggle? I didn't think so, but joining in is easy. Trying to stop something when everyone was part of it would be terribly hard, a job for a hero, a superhero, and I didn't think Y6 had one, whatever Tamsin said about needles and blood.

I did decide on a tactic, a simple one: smiling. I hoped I looked as if I had a special secret, but I knew I might just look as if I was "a few brain cells short of a *Big Brother* contestant" as Dad put it when someone was dozy. Daft. I don't suppose my smile was very convincing. In the playground it wobbled a bit.

That was the day I first saw George. He was in Y6Z and he'd been away the first week, but now that he was back he was impossible to miss. He was so much bigger than anyone else. He had spiky hair stiff with gel, ridged in the middle of his head like Table Mountain. He had a rolling sort of walk like a rodeo-riding cowboy with wide trousers that he didn't want to rub together between his legs. And his feet and hands were big enough for a man.

George was leaning against a wall, puffing because he'd been tearing around. His cheeks were red, but the rest of his face was as white as icing sugar. He wasn't wearing proper uniform and the shirt under his hoodie hung out over his trousers like the frosting sliding over the edge of the cake.

He seemed to be watching, his eyes taking in the whole playground. I didn't mean to watch him. I wouldn't have dared, not on purpose. I'd seen him chase the little ones and they weren't all enjoying it. He saw me looking and looked straight back. His stare was different, though, because he didn't seem to see anything funny. I didn't know what it meant, but I turned away.

The next thing I knew he was kicking a rubber ring, the sort that looks like a bagel. Then he was hooking it on his shoe, which was so big I thought it might get stuck. He bent down and picked it up, placed it on his head like a halo and faced me again. I don't know why he grabbed it, caught it and hurled it with an arc of a long, straight back arm onto the roof of the school. He was probably the only kid with enough reach and power to propel it there. That was when I noticed the other plastic colours and shapes, scattered across the tiles like a free, pop art pattern: balls and rings and a skipping rope, tightly rolled. It was quite a collection and the way he grinned made me think he was proud of it.

The lunchtime assistant in charge knew what he'd done, and shook his head, but he didn't go near George. Probably because he was like a great grizzly bear, and I think he knew it because I'd heard him roar at the little ones.

There were some plastic play tunnels in the playground. I thought they must be fixed because they didn't move and looked really heavy. They didn't budge an inch when anyone was inside them. But George charged at them, shoulders down, leaned in and pushed. There was a sharp, scraping sound as the tunnel shifted. The lunchtime supervisors all stopped still. One of them shifted too, towards George, but George kept shoving and heaving as if he was a one man battering ram with a whole castle wall to destroy. He cleared a good ruler's length, with black skid lines to prove it, before he was escorted indoors to the head's office. I remember wondering why George had bothered to do it, and why the grown-ups had bothered to mind. But then two little Y1 boys crawled out of the tunnel. One of them was crying, and had to be cuddled. Had George known it wasn't empty? If he hadn't, would he have cared?

At lunchtime I passed him, sitting outside the head's office, not allowed to go outside. And to my amazement, he winked. It was definitely meant for me, because I looked around in case there were some pretty girls behind me, but the wink was for me. I was too surprised to smile.

I asked Tamsin about him on the way home from school.

"Ugh! Keep away from him!" she said, making it sound like a warning in a fantasy story, as if he was some sort of ogre. I had already decided he was just a giant with no one to play with.

"Why?" I asked.

She wrinkled up her nose as if something smelled.

"Everyone does," she said. "He's soooooo weird. Yaz says his dad's in prison, assault probably. Or armed robbery."

Kay said he always walked to and from school on his own and had done for years. She had never seen his mother, not ever. She never went to parents' evenings or helped at school fairs or even joined the others for a girls' night out at Christmas.

"What you call a dysfunctional family," she added, looking left and right at a busy junction.

I wondered whether mine was dysfunctional too but when I asked Grandma over tea that day she said, "Oh no, dear!" She said it just had a little crack and that would soon be mended so you'd never notice it was there.

The next day Tamsin was ignoring me again because *their* crack seemed to be mended, even though I wondered whether the glue would be strong enough to stop it breaking apart again. Someone in her little group always seemed to be left out and crying. I reckoned friendships could be dysfunctional too.

At lunchtime George was standing on the wall. It was too high for anyone else to climb. He was standing on one leg and swinging the other.

"See?" he called as he saw me looking. "They're wrong. I'm not *off the wall.* I'm on it."

I knew what he meant, and I thought it was clever, but he explained it anyway.

"Crazy. Wacko. Screw loose. MAD!"

He wobbled his head as he said the last word and let his tongue hang out.

"Off the wall can just be different," I said.

He narrowed his eyes.

"Different," he repeated. "Like you."

"Yes," I said, looking at the church clock in case he was staring at my head and finding it funny.

"Why do you let them call you The Turnip?"

I stepped back as he jumped down from the wall. He was wearing tracksuit bottoms with a baggy, not very clean seat. He wiped his hands on it.

"I don't," I said. "I don't listen. I don't hear."

It wasn't exactly true but he seemed to be thinking about it.

"I get called The Blob," he said, "but not to my face." He said he didn't care, but he used words Mum wouldn't like. I wanted to tell him I didn't care either but somehow I knew he'd know it was a lie.

"You come to school with that Tamsin," he went on.

"Yes," I said, wondering how she'd feel if she knew it had been noticed.

"I call her The Bimbo. Or The Airhead. When it comes to your head, any head, it's better to have nothing on it than nothing in it."

I opened my mouth, and the words came out quickly, but they weren't very loud.

"She's good at maths," I said. "Quite good. She isn't thick."

"I say she is." George's words were slower and had much more volume. "Why are you arguing?"

I couldn't really tell whether he was angry or puzzled. I wasn't sure whether his target was changing from Tamsin to me.

"I'm just saying. She's…" I wanted to say my friend. She was the closest thing I had, nearer than London or Australia.

"As much use as sun block at midnight," he finished for me.

"She's all right," I said.

He didn't say anything then. He just kicked the wall a few times, gathering more and more force until he winced, gasped, hopped and grinned.

"What's your name anyway?"

"Daisy."

"Might get my head shaved, Daisy," he said.

I thought about it, and decided he was trying to be kind. Then he revved off, and his big cat purr widened into a growl I could still hear from the other end of the playground.

After that we spoke whenever we saw each other. He didn't smile, not exactly. But Tamsin said, as if it was a) impossible and b) not a good thing, that George liked me. I didn't mind. He was the only one, apart from Mrs Young, who seemed quite glad to see me every day. But I didn't tell Mum about him, not just because I thought she might agree about b), but because of a) too. When it came to weekdays I wasn't sure it was possible for either of us, George or me, to have a friend.

Chapter Eight

I told myself not to count on seeing Flame every weekend, because I knew he lived with his mum and that made things complicated. But I was so excited anyway that I hardly slept on that Friday night. So I wasn't in the best shape to deal with it when everything went wrong.

Dance class had been really good and Mum and the teacher said I was, too. We rushed back to find Dad waiting outside. They agreed that he'd stop for a cup of tea before we left for London and I was pleased to see them being friendly and polite. I didn't feel the storm coming; there were no warning signs.

When I heard the raised voices I edged into the kitchen end of the room, hoping they'd see me and stop. Dad had something in his hand and was leaning against the worktop. Mum had her arms folded and I knew that when she did that she wasn't just cross, she was holding herself up. As soon as I appeared the talking did stop, as if it had been sliced right through. Silence. But the anger carried on. I could feel it. The kitchen was still full of it five minutes later, after Dad had given me a quick kiss on the cheek, said he wasn't well and left without me.

I did see the photo on the worktop but I didn't take too much notice. I knew Dad had taken a picture the weekend before, when we were out by the river with Kyle and Flame. I'd been too happy to mind. After I'd stopped crying because I wasn't going to London, and telling Mum that Dad was a liar because he was never, ever ill, I looked at it. I was smiling. But it wasn't the smile I saw. It was my hair, my lack of hair. I looked almost completely bald. I felt my head to be sure and there were a few fuzzy patches, softer than they used to be. But the harsh light of the camera didn't register those wisps. It just bounced off my bumpy pink scalp.

I realised then that it was worse, much worse, than I'd really thought, because I'd stopped looking in mirrors. It was another tactic. And it had seemed like a good one.

But I didn't get it. What had happened between Mum and Dad? How could a photo have caused such a bust-up that either Mum wouldn't let me go or Dad didn't want me? His footsteps on the stairs had sounded as if he'd been running, as if he couldn't wait to get away.

"Never mind," said Mum. "We'll have a lovely time together. I'd be sad if you went to London every weekend."

"I want to go to Dad's," I said, pointlessly.

She just repeated the story about him being ill, and talked about swimming.

"Is there anyone you'd like to invite? Someone in your class? She could stay for tea …"

"No," I told her.

"Surely there's someone…"

"No," I told her, and I knew that made her sad, but I couldn't lie. It wouldn't work. And I wished I could swim with Flame because I imagined him gliding underwater like a merboy with his hair flowing behind him. I did think about George, who might be more like a manatee, but I didn't know where he lived. Besides, if he jumped in it would cause a tidal wave and a waterfall all at the same time.

In the end Mum gave up and invited Tamsin. I didn't want to go. I tried lying on my bed instead, but then Mum came in with my new silicone hat, which was swirly purple and pink, and modelled hers, which was bright sun yellow. I knew she was trying to make something of the weekend so I found my costume and towel.

Of course Tamsin refused to wear a cap even though Kay tried. She said swimming caps were skanky, and hurt her head, and smelt, and pulled her hair.

She didn't really like putting her head underwater and said the chlorine stung her eyes. It made her mascara run too. When the attendants put out the Arctic ice inflatable with the tunnels and holes to surface through, she seemed to think it was "baby" so I investigated it on my own.

After I'd swum miles and miles and she had mostly floated and trod water, Tamsin spent hours showering and shampooing while Mum and I waited. It took me about fifteen seconds to dry my head.

By early evening I felt exhausted, as if the tiredness wasn't just a heaviness in my limbs but deep inside me too. I told Mum I felt ill and went to bed.

"I must have caught what Dad's got," I said.

She tried to hug me but I pulled away, and when she came to check on me later I pretended to be asleep, even when she kissed my forehead very lightly so as not to wake me up.

I heard Mum call Auntie Sue. I heard the tears in her voice. I wanted to stop her, because I didn't want to hear it, any of it, whatever it was. But I rolled over and tried to actually sleep, and I must have done, because the next thing I knew it was late and Auntie Sue was on the landing, on the way out.

"I still can't believe him!" she was saying. "He's excelled himself this time."

"I've never really hated him before," said Mum, "not till tonight."

So I climbed out of bed. I headed towards the toilet, but what I really needed was to make them stop. Auntie Sue said an embarrassed hullo and Mum looked panic-stricken.

"What is it about the photo?" I asked. "Tell me."

Mum tried to put me off with words like "nothing" and "no need for you to worry," and "back to bed". But my eyes had widened out of sleep and I kept them fixed on hers. She didn't like looking back. She turned towards Auntie Sue as if she wanted help.

"You dad thought you might like to be a model, sweetheart, like Tamsin," said Auntie Sue.

"He thought it might make you feel better," said Mum. Her voice ebbed away to a trickle on an extra word: "Proud."

"I'll be off, Moll," said my auntie. I could tell she was in a hurry now.

"It was probably Sharon's idea," I said suddenly, "not Dad's."

Auntie Sue and Mum stared at each other. Auntie Sue stood still for a moment, and I could almost see through the tightness of her jaw that she was biting her tongue. Then she kissed Mum and was gone.

"I think it was Kay's idea, in fact," Mum told me, "but who is Sharon?"

So I told her. She looked pale in the light on the landing. All she kept saying was "I see." And I knew Dad had committed two crimes now: suggesting I did modelling and dating a hairdresser.

"It doesn't matter, because modelling is stupid and I'm proud anyway," I said. "And Dad is probably just lonely on his own."

Mum sighed a wobbly sigh and hugged me.

"I love you, Daisy," she said.

I didn't say I loved her too, because I was worrying about Dad.

And then he called me. My mobile rang just as I was trying to delete the scenes: the voices, the folded arms, the footsteps on the stairs.

"Daise?" he checked, as if a drug dealer might have stolen my phone.

"Hullo, Dad."

"Am I forgiven?"

I didn't know what for: the lost weekend, the row, the modelling or the Flamelessness. I realised that the photo at the centre of the tremor was the part I forgave first. It was just a mistake.

"I don't want to be a model with or without hair," I said, "but I know you were trying to celebrate my difference."

We had talked about celebrating differences at school. Mrs Young liked the words. She said them as if they had a lovely taste and I tried to say them the same way.

Dad was quiet on the other end. Then he said he was proud of me.

"I wasn't being insensitive," he said. "Well, no more than usual."

"I know," I said.

I said I'd tell Mum but he said not to bother.

"She doesn't hate you really," I told him.

"Ah!" he said. "That's reassuring."

It was tiring being a peacemaker and I wanted to sleep so I said goodnight and switched off my phone.

I didn't feel well on the Sunday. I really didn't: I had no energy. I didn't get dressed all day and didn't even read as much as I usually do when I'm poorly.

"I hoped you might come to church with me," said Mum, in the morning, sitting on my bed.

This was news to me. She never used to go to any kind of Sunday morning service when we were in the old house in the old town. I knew people asked God to make things better when they were sad. But He didn't. People died. People split up and had car accidents and bad illnesses. I liked the idea of a God that loved people and helped them to love each other but I knew there had always been sadness in the world and I thought there always would be. If there wasn't, how would we know when we were happy?

"Why do you go?" I asked her.

She looked thoughtful, as if I'd asked her a really difficult quiz question, but if she thought about it long enough she'd find the answer tucked away somewhere.

"Maybe," she said, "for some of that strength you've got." She paused. "I'm a bit short of it, you see."

"You're not," I said. "But you might be short of forgiveness."

She stared at me. I told her Dad didn't mean to upset anyone. She held her hands together on her lap for a moment. Then she stroked the top of my head.

"You're right. I'll work on it. I promise."

I wondered if she meant she would pray. I wondered if she prayed for me and my hair. I thought God had bigger things to worry about, but even so, I thought it was worth a try. There was a Bible verse about God counting the hairs on everyone's head, and even though in my case it wouldn't take Him long, I knew what it meant. Mrs Young had said. God cares about all of us, every little detail of us, more than anyone else. And I wanted to believe that. I wanted to remember it every time I saw Kevin Price's face looking at mine. It would help me not to think of him as the world's most horrible, stupid, heartless, evil person. I might even stop telling my diary that he was.

So Mum and I didn't go to church. But when the sun shone onto my bed although the air through the window was autumn cold, I wondered if God was in the light and the clouds. I knew Mum thought He was in the flowers someone brought her from the church. She brought them up to my room and stared at them, arranged like a picture on the window sill, as if she'd never seen anything so beautiful. Then she did an impression of the painting on my wall, called My Sweet Rose, and tried to breathe in the scent, close up, like a kiss. And I sprang out of bed and had a go myself, but there wasn't much smell, so I had to act the bliss. I think I overacted, because Mum laughed rather hysterically.

The weekend was coming to a slow and really quite peaceful end when my mobile rang again. His name didn't come up because I hadn't got him listed. But it was Flame. I sat up in bed and my book fell with a thud on the floor.

"Missed you," he said. "I made my dad get your number from yours but I said I'd be quick 'cos of the phone bill."

"Okay," I said. "Did you find the porpoise?"

"No," he said. "Dad thinks I imagined it because I wanted to see one. There have been loads of sightings …"

I heard Kyle call out, "Boy's OBSESSED!" and I grinned because I imagined him in his Cézanne apron with a hot pan of something wild steaming behind him.

"One day," I said, hoping I'd be there.

"But I nearly beat Dad down the hill."

I heard Kyle again, with a loud "In his dreams!"

"Mum's planning more direct action," Flame told me. "It'll really get noticed this time. Dad would do it too but I'd get taken into care if both my parents ended up inside."

"What about?" I asked, but I think Kyle was worrying about the phone bill again.

"Tell you soon," Flame said, "but I wanna know how school was. Any direct action on Kevin Price?"

I laughed and said school was bad. Ish. But I told him I was okay. It was true. Talking to him I really was, and when we'd said goodbye I wrote in my diary some forms the direct action on Kevin might take:

1. Decking him with a left hook. Not good because I would be suspended, Mum would be ashamed, and not in spirit of direct action anyway because it needs to be NON-VIOLENT.

Flame had told me. Gandhi started it. I was planning to google Gandhi when we got a computer.

2. Pulling his trousers down. Funnier but same problem with suspension and ashamed Mum.

I didn't think Gandhi would approve either.

3. Staging a demonstration. Problems: Where? Who would join in? Demos need crowds.

4. Writing a poem about bullying and making it so good Mrs Young reads it out and Kevin feels bad and stops. Not good because I'm not good at poems and Kevin's not good at feeling bad. Also rather INDIRECT action.

5.

The number sat on its own on the bottom of the list because I couldn't think of another. But as I lay ready for sleep I imagined number one, and Flame laughing at number two. I fell asleep listing embarrassing underpants Kevin might wear:

Thomas the Tank Engine
teddies
Bratz,
Victorian knickerbockers
Superman …
And I didn't feel so ill any more.

Chapter Nine

Things did settle at school for a while. Most jokes stop being funny in the end, even nicknames as incredibly witty as The Turnip. Every day I found a hair or two caught in my hairbrush, littering the wash basin like curly cracks, or left behind on the pillow. Of course everyone loses hairs each day, but the difference was that my body had forgotten how to grow new ones to replace the old. So as I got balder I was prepared. And it wouldn't have mattered so much what anyone called me if I felt I belonged, or if anyone except Nina ever chose me for a partner for anything. I thought Kevin would grow tired of looking at me as if I was an outbreak of mould or a flyblown cow pat. Or a clog of slimy, matted hair dug out from the plughole under the shower.

That was what Mum had to do by October, with our new shower. We'd moved into the house and I liked it. Mum and Liz had made it bright and cheerful in spite of all the grey days we were having and my bedroom had walls that were a dusky strawberry pink. Mum hung My Sweet Rose beside the sketch of Dad, so that I looked at both as I lay in bed.

So I had a new address. I also had what you might call a slightly lower profile, because there were days when Kevin didn't bother to give me the evil eye or call me ugly or a Martian or a geek or a nerd. Or even a sex object, which was the worst because it meant that no boy would ever fancy me even if I wanted them to.

"Girls shouldn't want to be sex objects," said Flame, when we were cycling on Wimbledon Common. Dad had bought me a second-hand bike. "It's like being a victim. Having no power. Being seen as an object, not a person. That's what Mum says."

"I think Tamsin wants to be one," I said.

"That's because the media control her mind," he said, and he asked if she read teen magazines or watched music channels.

"Only twenty-four seven!"

Flame had that look that means a case is proven, *open and shut, see?*

"Respect!" he said. "What you wanna be is the object of respect."

I knew Tamsin would rather be fancied than respected.

"I respect you," said Flame.

And I told him George did too. Flame reckoned George sounded awesome, until I told him about the headlines that went round the school, like Big Bear Terrorises Tinies. And the random acts of destruction.

"Not awesome then," he said. "Troubled."

George had been away again, but when he came back to school he'd been friendly, and he'd had a number one, which is the shortest haircut a boy can have, like a head of grass seed that's only just poking its way through. Exactly like that, in fact, because he'd dyed it green.

The headmaster, Mr Ogabe, sent him home. I didn't know why. George could still do maths and science and it wouldn't stop him heading the ball. I had an idea he had done it for me, but it didn't really work, because it didn't make him look like a Martian, even when it was supposed to be the right colour. It made him look mad and wild and, in a way, even bigger than he was. If he wanted to take over the role of freak he hadn't managed. That part was mine and no one else would get a look in.

Outside school there were other things to think about as Half Term approached. Not just a new home but what Mum called a rather surprising new development. Liz had met a man on the internet and after six weeks they had decided to get married. Mum and Auntie Sue thought it was the best, most romantic story since Romeo meets Juliet and nearly everybody dies.

I thought how good the story was would depend on the ending. Mum and Dad must have been a romantic story once. Anyway, it was great to see Mum smiling and believing there's such a thing as happiness because I knew she had found that hard for a while. We celebrated in the shop with a bottle of champagne that Kay had brought in, and after it had popped its cork to a lot of squealing and froth I was allowed what Liz called a splash.

"Why are you marrying him?" I asked, because I wanted to know.

"Because he's kind," she said, "and I decided that men can't be to blame for everything. Just war, and drips on the bathroom floor."

The two of them laughed so loudly that I wondered what they would be like by the end of the bottle. Then, when Liz stopped, long after Mum, she gave me a serious look.

"Would you be my bridesmaid, Daisy Waterhouse?"

I probably gawped.

"If I let you choose the fabric," she went on, "and the style, and made it myself?"

I had only just started to imagine the colours and the feel of a proper dress around my legs when I remembered, and my mouth opened into a "but" to follow the "Yes."

"If you want something completely stunning to wrap around that delicious little bonce of yours, we can design it together."

I smiled, because I knew it would be great, and no one would try to pull it off. And I started to feel quite excited.

I asked Flame whether he thought Liz was "off her trolley", which was Dad's opinion of both of them, Liz and her kind man. We were by the river, watching, keeping tally charts of everything that swam or flew or skimmed or paddled. Flame had borrowed his mum's camera too, and Kyle, who was having a beer with Dad in the pub garden a very loud shout away, had already accused him of being snap happy.

Flame considered Liz's decision for a moment. He didn't say she was "barking" (another one of the phrases Dad had used) and he pointed out that six weeks is a huge number of seconds.

"A lot can happen in a second," he said, "like seeing a porpoise and then losing it again. And the Dalai Lama says kindness is the only religion."

I said I liked that. Then I announced that kindness was the same as love without the snogging. (I hadn't enjoyed seeing Dad snogging Sharon on the sofa when they thought I was asleep.) Flame laughed. Then he wrote it down at the back of the notebook he was using for the tallying, as a quote in speech marks, with my name and the date at the end.

"Less slobbery too," he said.

We were kindness fans. But we knew someone who wasn't, and if it was a religion he couldn't belong. Unless, I supposed, the other worshippers were so kind they let him join anyway. There had been a man in the Bible who hated Christians and went round capturing them and throwing them in prison until he became one himself. Maybe Kevin could change. It didn't seem likely, but then neither did Liz agreeing to get married after six weeks. It's more than 3 million seconds, by the way, but that wasn't enough to change Dad's opinion that they were both "doolally tap".

After we'd chased each other around for a bit, Flame and I started to wonder about the living things we'd been looking out for in the river, and the ones we'd never find in Putney and whether they were kind.

"Everyone knows about penguins," I said, "and elephant mothers, but what about frogs and water boatmen and leeches?"

Flame was dipping the net again. We were taking turns. He was laughing at me again until he caught another bit of plastic in there, the kind of thing that holds four cans together and can strangle or trap the life out of something. We'd found a lot of rubbish already and he was starting to live up to his fiery name. He chucked it angrily into our bulging rubbish collection and dipped the net again.

And that was when we both saw a twisty, bumpy and ridged little creature, poking a snout out from the sludgy algae. It was so small we might almost have missed it in the midst of all the darting, swarming speck-sized species that were a thousand to the gram. And it was totally weird. It didn't look like a real life thing at all. It looked like something Liz would hang low from her ears. Something Tamsin would polish and clip on to her hair or her mobile – if she wasn't squirming at its grossness, because in an odd way it was just as ugly as it was beautiful.

What was lying in Flame's net didn't look like a fish to me, any more than it looked like a minibeast, even though it was beastlike, and very, very tiny. As well as a little snub snout, it had a kind of belly pouch that looked separate but attached, and more purply-red than the rest, which was rusty coloured, like blood that had dried. But there was a watery sheen to its whole, bulgy question mark of a body. On its back was a sort of fan shape with a yellow edge, the kind of thing a Spanish dancer would hold. And on its head it had a little bump, like a cartoon character who's been hit with a hammer. It was amazing and sci-fi and fantasy and I would have been jumping or squealing or whooping if I'd been able to take my eyes off it. Neither of us could. We just kept looking.

We hardly spoke at first. Flame was tilting the net a little bit, to slide off the gunk and get a clearer view. So it took a few moments to realise that it wasn't moving. In amidst all the chaos and speed of the rampaging life in that net, it just lay there, still as a stone and not much bigger than the kind that belongs, with a zillion others, to the gravel on a drive. But special. And incredible.

Flame and I stopped staring at it and stared at each other instead.

"Hippocampus," he said, because he knows these words, like Mum with chiaroscuro. It was a sea horse to me.

We hugged each other like goal scorers before we realised the glaringly, horribly obvious.

It wasn't just a slow mover, or pretending to be a bit of coral or something as a kind of tactic, so that no one would notice it. It was dead.

The dads must have realised from the pub garden, probably because of the roaring that went with the hug, that something had happened. They were hurrying towards us and mine was losing the race. By the time they reached us we didn't feel like celebrating any more, but we couldn't stop looking all the same.

"Whoah!" said Kyle.

"Is it real?" asked Dad, so I told him it was a brooch. Belonging to Dame Edna Everage.

"Niiiiiice," Kyle purred, stretching the word soft as fur.

"Would be," said Flame, who sounded upset now, "if it wasn't dead."

"Everything's gotta die," Kyle told him. "Think of it as a gift. Better than anything you'll find at Harrods."

I did. It was odd and different and peculiar and perfect. We took turns to lay it, very carefully, in the palms of our hands. It weighed almost nothing. Once the coating of water fell away through the gaps between my fingers it wasn't cold any more, but it wasn't warm either. I wanted to stroke it, but my finger seemed too large for the task. It would be like taking one of Dad's emulsion brushes to a drawing pin. It wasn't smooth and it wasn't rough either. And the more I looked at it, the more it seemed more magical than a fairy and just as hard to believe.

"Bit unusual, isn't it, in the Thames?" said Dad.

He can be embarrassing.

"Used to be unknown," said Kyle. "Not so long ago we'd be on *The News*. Not now. It's not the first. But it's ours."

Flame smiled at him. He was recovering.

"It's because there's more plankton now they've cleaned up the river," he told us. "And because of global warming too."

They had to explain that. Apparently seahorses are really a tropical or subtropical species, but our sea, and the river that feeds into it, is warmer now. I wished I had seen this one for a happier reason.

"They're sociable little guys," said Kyle, watching it in his own hand, where it looked even more miniscule. "And when they get excited they change colour. Like a shy dude dating for the first time, blushing. Only their blush is creamy yellow when they meet their mate." He grinned. "Romantic, hey?"

"Come on!" protested Dad. "You're winding us up."

"This expert from Project Seahorse," said Flame, "used orange tape to mark out the area she was studying, right? And one of the males went orange too."

This was so cool I was sure even Tamsin would love it. I remembered the camera and we took a shot each, just in case any of us missed, like when Dad cut the top off the grandparents' heads most Christmases. If we chopped off the smallest bit of hippocampus there wouldn't be a lot left. We knew the sea horse would come out a bit like a comma in the photographs because really to capture something that size we needed a BBC team with state-of-the-art equipment. But I was trying to seal it in my memory, fix it just as firmly as all the bad pictures that had set even though I didn't want to remember them at all.

I wanted to bury it with a sort of silent ceremony, but Flame said the river would be its grave so he asked me to throw it back. I wasn't sure how. Dad made a bad joke about skimming it like a stone and I glared at him. Then I cupped my hands, Flame tipped the net and I felt it land across the join in my palms, no heavier than a dog rose. Carefully I carried it a few steps to the water's edge, where I slid it in. And just for a moment I waited in case it gathered itself up into a thrust of living energy and swam away. It didn't. It bobbed on the movement of the small disturbance I had made. Then it rested like debris, and as I stepped back it became too small against the water and the sky, the buildings and the people, to do anything but disappear.

"Well," said Kyle, "That's something to talk about at school, yeah?"

I decided to email Jess in Australia. I wondered whether people in my class would believe me.

It was a special day and I was sad to say goodbye – to the river, to Flame, and then, when he dropped me off at the new house, to Dad.

"Come in and tell Mum with me," I told him.

"Okay," he said, and when I described the seahorse he joined in, not just backing me up but adding details and sounding as if he cared, and was excited too. I liked that and I could see Mum felt the same. She'd baked flapjacks, his favourites, and he ate three.

At bedtime, long after he'd gone, Mum said how much she wished she'd seen it too.

"Such a special thing, Daisy. Like a sign. It makes me feel hopeful. We've got a lovely new house, and Liz is in love. And," she paused, "I've sold a painting! For eighty pounds!"

"Wow!" I cried, but I was sorry when she told me it was the watercolour poppies because I'd miss them. "Who bought it?"

"Matthew," she said. "He runs the choir at church."

"Oh," I said.

I didn't know anything about Matthew then, but she told me even though I didn't ask. She said he was quite young, had a gingery sort of beard and used to be a bus driver. And wore red braces.

"We went out to tea today," she said, "in the café on the corner of the square. Lovely home-made scones."

"You won't be getting married in six weeks, will you?" I asked her, and something in my voice wanted to cry without giving my brain any warning.

"Oh, Daisy!" she said. "No! It was only afternoon tea. I'm telling you because of the painting and because I want to be open. That's all."

She meant Dad hadn't been open about Sharon. Of course, if I'd thought about it at all, it would have been obvious that somebody would be bound to like my mum. I just hadn't imagined it, and it felt uncomfortable. But she didn't think it was very likely that she would ever get married again.

"So don't worry."

She said it lightly, with a smile, but then she seemed frightened and wanted me to promise. I remembered what she'd said about the seahorse being a sign that things were going to get better. And I wondered whether better for Mum would automatically mean better for me. I told her I wanted her to be happy. But I knew that worrying isn't something you can promise not to do.

She rubbed the top of my head slowly and firmly, because she had a theory about getting the blood circulated. I tried to picture dark dot-like hairs under my scalp pushing up hard, like weightlifters, and breaking through, one after the other, until my head wasn't just speckly with shoots but thick with long, dark, shiny curls, rippling down. Until I was a Waterhouse girl.

"We have to believe," she said.

I wanted to. New hair, new friends, better dreams. So I nodded. But the seahorse was dead, and no matter how hard I tried as I closed my eyes, I couldn't make it swim, couldn't find the sunlight to dance off its tiny back.

In the morning there was a squashed bundle of hair lying like a puddle on the pillow and nothing at all on my head. Well, to be accurate, there was one longish, crinkly hair sprouting out above my ear, but it looked so lonely I yanked it out. Put it out of its misery. I felt all over my head, the smoothness of it, shiny and warm, but cooling fast in the morning air. I didn't mind the way it felt, the contours of it, the curves and dips.

I opened the wardrobe door and faced the mirror. I thought of babies and aliens. And I did feel a kind of shock, because this was a day that had taken its time to come but part of me never really believed it would. I don't know what I did expect, but not this. Not the completeness of it. I remember thinking it was kind of extreme and to the limit. And terribly real.

It wasn't that I minded the look of it, either, for myself. If you looked at my head as if it was in an art gallery or science museum, then the shape of me, with my small ears bursting out symmetrically like spring buds, was fun in a cartoonish sort of way. And in any case, what made me Daisy Waterhouse had never grown out of my head. But I wasn't sure that people, the ones who didn't love me, considered that. What they saw wasn't special, whatever Mum or Dad or Flame or Liz or George said. It was weird. And it wasn't a pretty sight.

I closed the wardrobe door, put on my uniform and tried to find my cap. It was cold out there.

Chapter Ten

The first thing Kevin did, after he'd arrived in the dinner hall and sat down facing Nina and me, was lean over and knock my cap off. I saw it happening a few seconds before it did because it was so predictable. The cap fell behind me, but I didn't follow its flight or check where it landed. I took no notice at all. I knew if I reached for it and pulled it back on, it would be like inviting him to play the game that toddlers love, when their mums put their shoes back on their little feet as they sit back in their buggies, and they kick them straight off again. So I just ate, but not as quickly as Nina. I wished I could tell her not to be frightened in words as well as with my eyes.

Kevin wanted to know if anyone had a spoon.

"To tap the egg," he said. Then he reconsidered. "Although usually I use a knife to slice the top off."

There were knives all around but I didn't expect him to pick one up. I was wrong. He found a dirty one, orange with baked bean sauce, and held it as if he was examining it. I looked down into my lunchbox. Then he put it down.

"Don't like egg really," he said. "Makes me sick."

One or two of the others made quite convincing retching noises. One of the dinner ladies came and asked them not to put people off their food. Kevin was eating. He wasn't devoting himself entirely to me. In fact he seemed to want me to see the contents of his mouth slopping around his teeth. Then he reached for an unused dessert spoon and tapped it on the table a couple of times. I pretended I wasn't paying any attention to him and was really enjoying my cheese salad sandwich. Nina just bolted her lunch down and sidled off with a sideways glance.

"See you later," she said, very squeakily.

Kevin blanked her. He always did. I kept chewing but the cheese was hard to swallow now. My mouth felt clogged and my jaw was stiff. I wasn't sure I could breathe and eat at the same time. Kevin had almost finished his mashed potato, thanks to the giant forkfuls he was shovelling in for my entertainment. The spoon was beside his plate, in a little orange puddle, but I didn't think he'd forgotten it.

He shuffled out of his chair, scraping it against the floor. He leaned in, and I thought he was going to pick up his plate to clear it away. But he picked up the dirty spoon and reached over to tap my head with it. I think I leaned away by instinct. I don't know, but it didn't make any difference because I felt it, cold and damp and hard on my scalp. He didn't strike me with it. It was more like the kind of measured beat you might give a triangle in a music lesson. It only hurt a little bit and for a moment. As his mates laughed he headed out of the room with a sudden turn of speed.

I used the paper napkin to wipe my head, reached for my cap on the floor, brushed off the salt from its peak and smelt it to make sure it didn't stink of ketchup or vinegar because I hate them both. I put it on my head and had a slow drink of water. Tears started to burn as I drank but I wiped them away before they could take hold. Then I went outside. I didn't want to be there. I'd rather have fallen into a hole and never climbed out again, but the playground didn't have any. And I didn't have any choice.

George found me about ten minutes later and knew straight away. I don't know how. My eyes were dry. Maybe he'd seen Kevin, who was probably still laughing.

"What did he do?"

I shook my head. I couldn't trust myself to stay dry if I tried to talk.

"Daisy?"

"Nothing," I managed. I knew he didn't believe me. "The usual," wobbled out.

George's large hands became claws as he shaped them in front of his chest like a Tyrannosaurus Rex.

"I'll flatten him," he said, teeth bared, and I pictured what Jerry does to Tom about ten times per minute, pancake thin on the floor or wall. I was laughing then, at George, and the splatted cartoon cat in my head. It was the kind of laugh that sometimes lapses into crying but covers it up quite well.

"You think I'm kidding!" he cried. "But I will. If he doesn't leave you alone I will!"

"You won't," I told him. "They'd expel you. And it would be my fault. And it's okay. It's nothing."

"Kevin Price is nothing," he said. "Rien! Zilch. He doesn't exist."

"Kevin who?" I said, so he laughed and charged off as if he was a remote control car and somebody had just pressed a button. He careered around like one too, changing direction suddenly and revving off again.

Then Nina came over and invited me to go to her house the next day, for tea. I knew she felt guilty, and wished she wouldn't. It wasn't her fault and I didn't want her to feel sorry for me.

Diary entry: *I HATE KEVIN PRICE. Kevin Pig. Kevin Rodent. Kevin Hyena. Kevin who who who who WHO?*

The next day Nina looked awkward and said sorry twice before she explained that her mum had said no. That was all, but then her English still wasn't up to a lot of detail.

"Sorry," she said, again.

"It's okay," I told her. "Come to mine sometime. My house."

She liked that idea. I could see it in her eyes, which were usually washed pale, like the beginning of one of Mum's watercolour skies.

"Thank you very much, Daisy," she said. "That be very nice."

She always spoke very softly, in case she made mistakes, but her voice had a crisp sort of edge. It was the right sort of voice for her, because she was so small and thin and her face never looked flushed even after P.E. I knew she wanted to fade into every background. If she'd been a sea horse she would have turned green on the field and dark blue like our school sweatshirts in the classroom.

Mum said maybe she could come over during Half Term. I wondered about asking Tamsin round at the same time so that she could do some of the talking, because I knew Nina wouldn't do much herself. The trouble was that I wasn't sure Tamsin would bother to talk to Nina. I mentioned it on the way home, in Kay's car.

"Nina?" she echoed, as if I'd suggested inviting a toddler from Reception, or a newt. "What for?"

"She's nice to me," I said, "and she hasn't got any friends."

It did cross my mind that the two things might be connected, but it couldn't be easy settling in England if you'd come from Poland for a better life and hadn't really found one.

"She's weird," said Tamsin, as if there was a bad smell in the car.

"No she isn't," I said. "You'd probably seem weird in Poland."

George would have said she wouldn't have to go that far and imagining that made me smile.

That was the afternoon I finally got an answer to the question in my head about Tamsin, but it wasn't the one I wanted. I did notice, even on the back seat of the car as we talked, that her bag was full. I didn't guess. Not until later on, at her house, when she was making a pop-up heart-shaped card for a boy, even though it wasn't nearly Valentine's, and produced some red tissue and shiny ribbon from the bag, along with a brand new stick of glue, some glitter and sequins. She was so focused on every detail of the card that she didn't seem to expect me to ask and I didn't. I knew she'd taken them from the stock cupboard at school, because Mrs Young had asked the two of us to put some paper back on the shelves in there and we'd seen it all there.

"They sell all those things in The Art House," I said.

"Yeah?" she said, as a question.

"So your mum can afford to buy them."

"I wanted them today," she said, as if that was good enough and it was nothing. As if I was the one with the problem.

"It's stealing," I said.

"So?" she huffed, impatient with me and with the fiddliness of attaching the sequins, which were trying to lodge themselves in her long, French manicured nails. "It's paper. And glue. Not a D and G handbag or Gucci shoes."

She collected names like that. I just hadn't realised she collected other things too. But her mum came in then, and she shoved everything under a cushion really quickly. I found myself smiling guiltily at Kay as if I'd done something wrong. I didn't know what to do. Tamsin was hardly going to stop stealing because I told her she shouldn't. So I added it to the list of things I couldn't tell. This time I couldn't even offload on Flame, because he would be away for Half Term with his mum and little brother. I'd almost burst into tears when Dad told me that.

Of course I was glad to have a week away from Kevin Price, because however much I liked the lessons and Mrs Young and George, it was hard not to hate school when he was there. There was talk of me going to stay with Dad's parents just for the weekend and then with my grandparents on Mum's side for most of the week. I didn't mind, but there would be no one my age around and I was worried that Grandma would take one look at my head and cry.

Then Dad rang.

"Twinkletoes!" he cried, so I could tell he was very pleased about something. "I'm on the net booking a holiday and I want you to come."

"Yeah!" I said.

"Daise, look," he began, and I worried instantly. "I know you don't approve of flying but we can't get a train to Lanzarote. Or cycle. It's a cheap deal which is all I can afford. A week in the sun. Lovely white sand. Three pools. Dramatic volcanic rock and spectacular caves." He paused. "Go on, say yes. It'd be a break together, the two of us."

I wished he wouldn't do it to me. He was making out that my principles were blocks, obstacles, interfering with fun and happiness and sunshine. And our relationship, father and daughter. It wasn't fair.

I asked if we could go somewhere else but according to Dad wherever we went in this country we'd go down with hypothermia and spend the whole week in kagoules with the hoods tied tightly against downpours and gale force winds. Besides, he said, he couldn't afford it. Lanzarote was cheaper. I said it shouldn't be and the government should sort things out so that people didn't use money as an excuse to harm the environment. He went silent then and I knew I'd upset him. I heard him sigh.

"Honestly, Daise, you can be such a killjoy," he said, quietly. "Aren't things miserable enough?"

I didn't know whether he meant for him or me. He'd seemed happy enough with Sharon on the sofa. I wasn't going to admit that things could sometimes feel quite miserable for me, especially at playtimes. I wanted to be the brave, upbeat me that Flame respected.

"I'm okay," I said.

"Right," he said, and I could tell he didn't know what to say. We both waited a moment or two. Then he told me I'd taken the wind right out of his sails.

"Sorry," I said.

"Don't say sorry," he said, "say yes. For me."

"All right," I said. "I'll come."

And he whooped on the other end of the line. I could imagine him making one of those footballer fists that he liked to pull down, just like the boys in my class.

"That's great, Daise," he said, and he sounded mushy then. I wondered whether his eyes were clouding, and I realised I'd made him happy.

It did occur to me to ask Flame whether his mum was planning any more direct action at airports. I wanted to meet her one day, but not like that, when she was climbing up on the roof of a plane with a banner, watching me climbing into another one in shorts and flip-flops, keeping my head down in a spotty sunhat.

Mum said that head would need protecting. My scalp mustn't burn. She hoped, as a veggie, I'd find enough to eat out there. My grandparents would be disappointed. And she'd miss me.

And was the holiday for two?

I stared. I hadn't thought. Surely Dad would have said.

"Of course," I said.

I didn't hate Sharon any more than I hated the Prime Minister or the headmaster of my school, but that didn't mean I wanted a week on the beach with any of them.

Luckily, I didn't think Sharon would want a week on the beach with me, either, drawing attention of the wrong kind. I knew people would stare, and talk about me in Spanish. But as long as nobody grabbed my sunhat or tapped me on the head with a spoon, I decided not to care.

The flight attendants didn't do either of those things. They were so kind that I asked Dad to tell them I hadn't got cancer.

"I can't do that!" he objected, keeping his voice down even though he usually spoke much too loudly and the passengers eight rows back must have thought his so-called jokes were for them.

"They're sorry for me because they think I'm dying and I'm not," I said, "so you have to tell them or I'll feel really bad."

"We'll get it put on a T-shirt when we get to Lanzarote," said Dad, "in seven languages."

But he did get up and have a quiet word with the oldest female, who looked at me with such a sweet smile I wondered whether she felt even sorrier for me now. When he sat down again he reported that she'd said I was a very brave girl.

"I'm normal, that's all," I muttered at my book.

"Oh, Daise, come on!" Dad grinned. "You've never been that!" He elbowed me in his friendly, *just a joke* way. Then he looked serious. "You've always been much bigger, much better than that."

I smiled, and he held my hand for a moment.

"It's going to be a great holiday," he told me.

"Didn't Sharon want to come?" I asked, eyes on the book.

Even though I wasn't looking I knew Dad had turned to look past me out of the window.

"Yes," he said, and paused, "she did. But I'm not seeing Sharon any more."

"Oh," I said.

I held his hand that time, in case she had hurt him, and he gave it a squeeze. The way he grinned, as if Tottenham had just gone a goal up against Chelsea, he didn't seem too wounded.

"You're worth ten Sharons," he said. "Twenty."

I was glad he thought so, but I did wonder what Sharon had done.

I was quite excited by the time we climbed out of the plane. I decided straight away, as our bodies soaked up the heat, that the temperature in Lanzarote was perfect for me. It wasn't so hot that my scalp would burn red and blister if I felt safe enough to go bareheaded, but under my hat it didn't run with rivers of sweat. Once we arrived at the resort and explored the balcony, I let breeze blow softly around my head. I loved the way it stroked me.

Of course I loved the water too. We were in the sea within fifteen minutes of arriving at the hotel, even though the beach was lined with towelled sun loungers by then and we were close enough to the nearest family to learn a lot of German. They were close enough to get plenty of good, long looks at my head, too, but I was used to stares. Dad behaved like a five-year-old, shrieking when I splashed to encourage him into the water and hopping as if he had been bitten by a jellyfish. As we swam further out, fish gathered below us, darting, gleaming and crowding. Dad seemed to be heading for Morocco. Every now and then he waited, arms folded like an angry headmaster as he trod water, shouting things like, "Come on, Dozy! What's the matter with you?" or "Is this the best you can do?" or "Told you to give up smoking!" Which made it hard for me to keep up because I was laughing, even though he wasn't funny.

I caught him smoking that night, outside on the balcony that crossed both our rooms, when he thought I was asleep. I could only see the back of him in his creased holiday shirt and baggy shorts but he looked different. Not just smaller, but unplugged. No spark. And I wanted to tell him he didn't have to pretend to be happy and mad all the time, just for me.

We went on a tour on the third day and saw some cool rocks that had once been lava. You could see the curves of the pouring liquid, set solid and black. There was a cave with amazing colours, and another one where the guide took us to the edge of a sudden drop. He told us how dangerous it was, how careful we must be, and how we must take a look one by one, with him right there to grab if we were frightened. He picked me for the first go.

"Don't jump, Daise!" called Dad, helpfully.

Just a ruler's length away from me the rock fell away, down and down, sheer and deep enough to make anyone take a quick step back with a wobbly head. It was the sort of chasm even Indiana Jones would think twice about swinging down. My mouth opened and then pulled wide in a sort of cartoon terror face as I turned to Dad. It was his turn next and as the guide beckoned him he cried, "Whoah! Vertigo!" and took my arm. But then the guide took a pebble, smiled, told us to listen and dropped it. We were all expecting it to plummet down, down, DOWN for ever before it landed at the bottom five miles down, but all we heard was a little plop. The guide was grinning broadly as if the joke was equally funny with every set of gasping tourists. There was no chasm, just a pool of water, reflecting the rock above.

"Nice trick!" Dad told him, and I hoped he wasn't going for a high five.

He kept asking me, over the first few days, whether I was having a good time, and I was. We were getting through a lot of sun cream on my head because it wasn't really worth holding on to hats when the wind blew off the sea, but I was feeling safer now. Toddlers pointed as if they had seen a dog with eight legs or a beach ball with fangs. Teenagers muttered to each other. But I didn't know them; they didn't know me.

I beat Dad at ping pong four times out of nineteen. I got better and better at snorkelling. We played beach cricket on a round-the-rock stretch of sand we'd found, where there was plenty of space because it was a long walk from any bars. We tried to name the fish, but we couldn't count them because they were too quick, bright and twisty in the sunlight.

Mostly we'd tired ourselves by the time we'd finished supper, and Dad usually pretended he couldn't walk after lots of bread, potatoes and pasta and creamy dessert washed down with beer. But when we were walking/staggering back to our rooms one night, enjoying the darkness because it was so warm and smooth, we heard the kind of music Dad likes best: the New Romantic stuff he bought when he was young. There was a live band playing at the cocktail bar by the largest pool, and a short Spanish man with curly black hair and a flowery shirt was singing. Dad's mouth opened in delight. It was the opening bar of "Don't you want me baby?" which was Dad's all time favourite song. He grabbed my hand and dragged me out to the shiny floor where a few couples were doing the kind of dancing where you hold on to each other's waists and stay upright. One woman turned her head so far to take a really good look at me that I thought it might twist right off. Dad gave her a little wave when I knew he'd rather give her a piece of his mind. Like the other couples, she was jiggling from the waist, but slowly, half-heartedly, as if now that she had recovered from her shock she was in a kind of trance.

Dad and I don't do half-hearted when we dance. He has his moves and they're different from mine, or anybody else's. They use a thumb and an elbow, and tilting from side to side as if he's surfing and trying not to fall, and there's a magic spell thing that his hands do in front of his face from time to time. But this time we danced together, with jivey arches and twists and pull-throughs, and I don't know where the steps came from but we seemed to know what to do next. By the end of the song I was laughing and Dad was exhausted. He wanted to sit down and have a drink but I wasn't ready. I was having way too much fun. Something took hold of me and I felt as if I was fizzing with energy that would never run out. I made everything up as I went along but it all fitted together somehow. It felt fast and light and all the time the colours on the water danced too, like jagged brushstrokes shining. And Dad took my lead and followed, sort of, with an expression of determined concentration on his face.

As the music stopped there was a lot of clapping and cheering and some of it was coming from the band. It took me a moment to realise it was for me. Dad said, as we walked away, that he was proud as punch, and I told him to shhh because he was shouting. But before I went to bed I thanked him for a brilliant holiday.

On the last night there was a talent contest for under 16s. As soon as Dad saw the notice he became obsessed. I must enter. I'd cane! I only agreed in the end to please him, after I'd run out of ways to say no. We had a lovely, relaxed final day, both of us reading, but chatting too, and enjoying our last attempt to reach Morocco by front crawl. By the time the evening came I was almost looking forward to doing my dance. I'd run through it a few times in Dad's room while I sang the accompanying music myself because he just couldn't remember the right words and when he got them wrong I couldn't dance for laughing.

The show was by the largest pool. There were about eight contestants, mostly familiar, although none of them had ever spoken to me (only about me). They included a tall, long-faced boy who had greased his hair flat and stuck a spotty bow tie round his neck because he was the comedian. Tamsin would have called him a nerd in spite of the Nirvana T-shirt. And there was a little blonde seven-year-old called Alicia whose hair sprang into curls like those bows on parcels that you make if you stroke the ribbon with a scissor blade. She was going to sing. Her mother, who was so agitated she seemed short of breath, kept repeating tips as if Simon Cowell might be in the audience.

As soon as her mother had been asked to go and sit down by the holiday rep in charge, Alicia started to cry. I asked her if she was all right.

"I always get nerves before performing," she said. "Sometimes I throw up."

"Nice," said the Nirvana comic. "Lay off these shoes, will you?"

He was wearing plimsolls with holes in the toes and one was sprouting a plastic flower he must have taken from the bar. I smiled, but he gave me the wrong kind of smile back.

"Can I give you a shout if I need funnier material?" he asked. "You'd only have to walk on."

I looked down at my own feet. That week I'd almost been forgetting, at times, what people saw. I'd got used to me. But strangers didn't get the chance, and when I saw myself again through their eyes, it was a shock all over again.

"Just a joke," he said, sounding nervous and moving away because the show was about to start.

The standard of the acts wasn't what you'd call high quality. Flame would have laughed himself silly. Tamsin would have scrunched her nose up to her forehead through every act. George might have wanted to throw something, or someone, high onto the roof.

In the end I felt sorry for the comedian because he just wasn't very funny. His jokes were the kind they put in crackers, like *What do you call a deer with no eyes? No idea,* and *An orange and a banana came into the bar and the banana said, "You're round."* Except that the first time he told it the orange told the banana he was round and the second time, when he got it right in his slow, news reader voice, even his mum and dad didn't laugh. I remembered something I'd heard about comics often being depressed off stage. This boy seemed pretty depressed when he was on.

When it came to her turn, Alicia stretched her long thin arms out of her shiny ra ra dress and opened her mouth so wide that an enormous noise burst out. Dad said afterwards it would have made paint crack on walls. Her mother stood up to clap and I thought she'd probably win, because her voice was so much bigger than she was.

I just danced. It wasn't the song I asked for but I improvised, even though everyone must have been sick of hearing it because of the hot, hot, hot chorus that beat round the pools every day anyway. I felt a bit embarrassed at the end and wished Dad had taken no for an answer, but he wasn't the only one who clapped loudly, although nobody else actually whistled with two fingers and stamped their feet under the table.

The winner would be announced, said the rep with the microphone, after the judges had taken a few minutes to confer, so we should all get another drink in. I went to the toilet. When I came out to wash my hands, there was Alicia by the paper towel dispenser. Her make-up had smeared and her curls were starting to nosedive in the heat. Her mother didn't see me, because she was bending down to her and consoling her, brushing her dress and wiping her mascara. She was telling her she'd been wonderful but Alicia said she was never entering another talent contest again, ever, and her mother couldn't make her. Her lip wobbled and she started to whimper, which made her mum very flustered.

"It isn't a fair contest anyway, sugar," she told her, just as I pushed the door and left, rubbing my wet hands on my shorts. "They're bound to let the bald girl win."

I don't know why it felt the way it did, like something inside tightening and tearing. I just ran, out to the poolside and past the tables and chairs, the breaking lights juddering in the water as if I was shaking them. I didn't go over to Dad because that would have meant threading through people. I knew he'd see me and follow but I didn't want to look at his face or anyone's. I tripped on a sharp stone, fell and cut my knee but started running again, just not so fast. At the door to my room next to Dad's I waited, blood shining down my leg in the light above the number, waiting.

He made a lot of noise with the key but he didn't speak. Unless you count a word, a question, that I didn't answer though he asked it again and again: "Daise?"

Inside the room, he got some wet loo roll and wiped my leg. His hand was shaky. My leg ran with blood and sandy dirt thinning into a watery trickle.

"You won," he said, with no fist and no whoop, and I cried.

Chapter Eleven

Of course I recovered. I didn't take the diary to Lanzarote and I can't be sure, now, what the wild words would have been. Volcanoes lie quiet for decades, centuries. Then they erupt and people run for cover. I know a counsellor would say I'd been too quiet, kept too much inside. Maybe I needed to explode instead of cry and cry and cry. But the crying was the closest I got and it was hard to tell Dad what I felt or why.

He was quiet, by his standards, on the journey back to England. We both were. I told him I'd used up my tear allowance and there was a shortage now all over Spain. I had to keep telling him it hadn't spoiled the holiday and I couldn't help overreacting but I was all right now.

"Why did you split up with Sharon?" I asked him, in the car heading home. He was eating boiled sweets and his sucking was typically loud.

"Oh, no reason," he tried, but I knew it was to do with me, so I pushed.

"For a hairdresser, she wasn't very sensitive about you," he said, "and she wanted the two of us to go on holiday."

"Without me."

"Yes. She hasn't got kids. She doesn't understand."

"You can find a nicer girlfriend," I said, "but maybe not so pretty."

He smiled.

"Ah," he said. "Beauty is in the eye of the beholder."

That means that if you love someone he looks gorgeous to you. Or that Dad thought I was beautiful even though I never had been, and couldn't be, not now.

"I had a much better time with you," he told me.

I wasn't sure about that because Sharon would have let him smoke, but I decided to believe him.

Of course I told Mum that bit of news and she made a little noise through her nose which meant she didn't like Sharon one bit even though she hadn't met her. I told her all the best things about the holiday and the worst too, which made her hate Alicia's mother even more. I emailed Jess to tell her I'd had a fab time, but Jess only replied that her mum was having a baby (smiley face, kiss, kiss). She sounded really happy and I thought she would probably forget about me soon.

I had asked Dad to say hi to Flame through Kyle. I wished I could tell him everything, apart from the crying, because if he knew about that he might not respect me so much. And I could have told him that I wasn't looking forward to going back to school, even though the second half of term led up to Christmas and I liked plays and shows, making decorations and singing carols. November had just begun and Mum had bought me a couple of woolly hats. My favourite had flaps and pompoms but I couldn't really wear it in class, not if I wanted to hear a word Mrs Young said.

Actually she said a few interesting things on that first day back. One: it would be Parents' Evening soon. I was a bit worried that between them Mrs Young and Mum might work out more than I wanted them to know. Two: she would be casting the Christmas production soon. It would be scenes from *The Lion, the Witch and the Wardrobe,* using music and dance, and all her idea of course. I thought it sounded brilliant because I love Narnia and I hoped, because I knew she liked my dancing, that she might put me down for more than first tree or even second wolf.

She did ask me quietly whether I felt more settled at school now.

"Oh, yes," I lied. "Thank you."

"You seem to be getting on with Nina," she'd noticed.

"Yes," I said, "she's coming to tea," which was true, because over Half Term Mum had managed to get her mum's phone number and arranged it.

"That's great," said Mrs Young. "Nina could do with a good friend."

Teachers can't make children like someone. They can talk about being kind, and have school values like sharing and listening and being considerate, but they can't make anyone be nice to someone else if being nasty seems to be much more fun. I know now that I should have talked to her about Kevin, but I had an idea that the bravest thing to do was to deal with it myself. I thought that eventually my bravery would make him stop. But that's something I shouldn't have counted on.

I wasn't sure Tamsin was someone I could count on, but she was being much friendlier, and at the end of the day I found out why. Nina was with us but Tamsin acted as if she wasn't there.

"That George told me you said I'm not a bimbo," she said, "and stuck up for me. He said I should stick up for you."

"Oh," I said. We were looking out for Kay's car near the school gates.

"He's scary," she said, and shuddered.

"Not really," I told her. "He just doesn't know how to fit in."

"Well he's soooo massive!" cried Tamsin. "If he wants to fit in anywhere he shouldn't eat so many pies."

I told her that wasn't fair because he was tall more than fat. She supposed so.

"George is big bear," said Nina in her small voice and I agreed, but said his claws weren't sharp. I had to show her that with an impression which made her laugh.

"Oh," said Tamsin, "Gemma gave me this for you."

It was a party invitation, my first. I thought I might not go, because I'd rather see Flame, but that wasn't the point. I'd been asked. Although I wished she had given it to me another time, because it made it obvious that there wasn't one for Nina.

Tamsin hung around for a while with Nina and me, but when we both said we didn't want to watch MTV all evening she went home. Nina looked at the doorway after she'd been through it.

"So pretty," she said.

"You too," I told her, because when she smiled she was. Not like a princess or movie star, because she still looked like a Victorian urchin, the kind of waif the Happy Prince gives up a jewel for in the story, but pretty in a delicate way, because of the interesting things inside her.

She looked at me as if I'd just given her enough money to bring over all her family from Poland and buy a mansion for them all to share.

"You best girl in school, Daisy," she said. "Why you got no hair?"

I looked at her, wondering what to say, wondering what Mum would say, or Dad, and whether it would be the same. I wasn't sure she'd understand stress or even divorce but she'd certainly know about moving and a new school.

"Maybe because of all the changes in my life," I said, "and not being very good at handling them." She seemed to understand. "Or maybe because I'm a turnip."

It turned out that Nina didn't know what a turnip was, but I found one in the vegetable rack and showed her. She said Kevin was a "bad boy". Then I asked Mum if we could boil two eggs as a kind of starter and when they were cooked but cold enough, we both had a go at turning them into Kevins, with spiky yellow hair felt tipped on. Nina blacked in his teeth and I gave him big red spots all over his face. Then we said "One, two, three!" and sliced the tops off with our knives at the same moment. It wasn't really as funny as it felt.

Nina said that before I joined the school he picked on her. I should have known. Before Mum and I walked her home she said she would persuade her mum to invite me back but her flat was "not nice like your house". When we arrived at the block of flats Nina buzzed, but although she tried to press the outside door it did not open. We waited until her mother came down with her keys in her hand and said thank you about five times. She looked like Nina, but her hair was grey and tied back tightly. It made her forehead look wide and tired.

"I shouldn't feel too sorry for myself, should I?" said Mum, as we left. "I would have suggested meeting for coffee one day, but when would she have time for that?"

On the walk I told Mum that I'd had my best day at school so far and she hugged me. She hugged me again two days later after Parents' Evening because Mrs Young had told her I was bright and talented and a lovely girl too. Mum said she was even prouder of the loveliness than the brains and talent and it was great to see her looking happy.

And the next day Mrs Young asked me to be the White Witch in the Christmas production. I was *amazed*, my diary said, *shocked, gobsmacked and stunned*! More than that, I was bursting with a kind of joy I hadn't felt for a while. She said her only worry was that I was too nice to be able to act so nasty but I said I'd manage, and showed her a twisty motif with my body, right down to my spell-casting fingertips.

"Okay," she said, pretending to be scared, "I'm not worried any more. I'm terrified!"

Maybe if Mrs Young had given me a small part like Kevin, who actually was third wolf at the Stone Table, taking orders from me as White Witch, he would have got tired of me. He might have looked around Reception for someone with big ears or a lisp. As it was, he decided to stick with me.

It was Friday break time. I'd seen him and his mates gather around Gemma and Tamsin, who glanced in my direction more than once. I guessed he wanted to know why anyone would invite a turnip, or an egg, to a party. Gemma was shrugging a lot, as if she didn't care, but I could see she didn't like it. No one liked that kind of attention from Kevin.

Then he left the girls, looked round and saw me. Maybe he knew where I was all along. I noticed he had something bulging in his pocket and I had an idea it wasn't a ball. He showed it to his friends, making sure I couldn't see anything except their laughter. When they looked across to me they laughed even more. I thought about going to the toilet, but running away and hiding would be a first and I didn't want to start, not now that I was feeling better about everything.

"Shut your eyes, Daisy," he called as he drew closer, the thing back in his pocket. "I got a present for you."

I didn't shut my eyes, or put out my hands, but he pushed it into the pocket of my coat. It felt solid, and quite heavy. Nina edged away. I didn't blame her.

"Have a look and see if it reminds you of anyone," he called, and stepped back to watch what happened next, because he thought I'd look. I didn't want to. I let whatever it was weigh down my pocket. But then I panicked, and he was counting on that. He was counting on me having to know.

I tried to move to a more private place to find out but Kevin and his mates just followed me, parallel, never too far away. So I pulled it out. It was a turnip with an ugly face drawn on, and below that, two big, saggy breasts and a tummy button. One breast had a D on it, and the other a W.

I was burning in my eyes and cheeks and chest. I stared at it, kept my eyes on it, didn't want to look up. There was snorting and snuffling. His audience loved it. And I did think about treading on it, but I wasn't sure I could squash it and I didn't fancy giving them more fun by failing and hurting my foot. If I'd had giant, thick-soled trainers like the pair I saw down in front of me now ...

George held his big hand out. I gave it to him, but even though I was glad to see him I didn't manage a smile. He ran straight towards Kevin, who dodged him, until he swerved and faced the school roof. Up it went, past the guttering, and lodged not far from a small ball.

"Oh yessssss," he murmured to himself, like a hiss.

The bell rang. Kevin looked relieved, until George brushed past him and whispered something hard in his ear. Tamsin told me a couple of minutes later in the corridor that George had to stay in at lunchtime again for calling Kevin something a lot worse than a turnip.

I know that was when I should have told, but what difference would it have made? George had thrown something else on the roof and used a swear word. He would stay in anyway, and I suppose I was glad, because I didn't want any more trouble between them. I just wanted to forget it and go back to feeling better.

So it was a shock, at lunchtime, to find that rather than sitting outside the head's office, George was hiding under the fire escape steps that led up to the hall.

"Call him over," he whispered.

I knew who he meant because Kevin and his friends were studying football stickers not far away.

"Why?" I wanted to know.

"Go on, call him. He'll be so shocked he'll come."

"No," I said. "Why?"

"Call him princess. He hates that."

"No ..."

It was the nickname he knew George had given him, because his hair was quite long now, and rather beautiful. How would I dare?

"I'm not going to hurt him."

So I called. I called him Kevin first, so quietly he didn't hear. Then I tried again: "Kevin! Princess!"

I bet he couldn't believe his ears. He looked away from the stickers and realised it was me. His mouth widened so far he could have been at the dentist and his fair eyebrows almost kissed. He had never looked at me like that. He was so angry he didn't know what to do with himself except come. I don't think he had worked out what he would do or say to me.

When George pulled Kevin from behind, his arm locked round his neck, I gasped. I think I said "No!" but maybe I only thought it. George must have had some scissors in his pocket, because while he held him still with his left arm, his right hand was busy cutting through a great blond gathering of hair that fell down across Kevin's forehead. Then he grabbed another handful and cut that too. And another. His scissors must have been sharp because the hair fell so quickly. Kevin was squirming and groaning but it was all happening under the steps that blocked the view of the lunchtime supervisors chatting over coffee. No one would know unless someone told, and that couldn't be me, could it, not when George was doing this for me?

Kevin's struggling had edged them closer to the concrete slope that was the base of the fire escape. George was still snipping and fair hair was streaking the puddles. I don't know how it happened then. Maybe Kevin was reaching for the scissors and George jerked him away. It was hard to see. I didn't want to see. But however it happened, or why, Kevin's head knocked the concrete. Not George's, even though he was a whole foot taller, but Kevin's, with a thud, a sharp one, that made George let go. And made me catch my breath. It was horrible. There was Kevin, bleeding, dropping to his knees, holding his head, seeing the blood gush through his fingers and splash the ground. He was screaming so loudly it hurt to hear him. George covered his ears as if he couldn't bear the crying, his head hunched on his shoulders. He dropped the scissors and they landed in a puddle.

We were surrounded now. Kevin's mates were shouting. The lunchtime supervisor sent for the head. George looked drained and crumpled at the waist. His face was red, but white was seeping through. He didn't run. He didn't move.

Fifteen minutes later Kevin was being driven off to Casualty in an ambulance and George really was waiting outside the head's office, waiting for his mum to take him home. I was inside the office, and saw her arrive, a towering woman with enormous feet. She didn't look angry, but she looked very sad, just like Mum would be, very soon.

When they had gone it was my turn. I cried so much I couldn't speak for ages. Mr Ogabe asked me where the scissors came from and I said I didn't know. I was finding it so hard to breathe he checked that I didn't have asthma. One of Kevin's friends had said I gave George the scissors. Did I? Had I told George to get Kevin? I shook my head and cried but even the word 'No' was hard to heave out, and when it came it was in a breathy rush. I was afraid of the sound of it.

I saw Mum step out of Liz's car. I couldn't bear to imagine what she was thinking. I had never been in trouble. I had been her lovely girl. She almost ran to the door, and when Mr Ogabe asked her very calmly to sit down, she hugged me first. So I knew, as she held me for that moment, that she understood I hadn't meant it, any of it, to happen.

She listened to what he told her, which wasn't much and mostly about Kevin. She sat with one hand running fingers through the other. She dropped her bag and picked it up again.

"I'm very sorry indeed that this boy has been hurt, Mr Ogabe," she said, "but Daisy cannot be to blame. Not in any way."

"That may very well be the case, Mrs Waterhouse," he said, "and all we are doing is trying to establish the facts."

"That is a fact," said Mum. "Daisy has never hurt anyone in her whole life."

It wasn't completely true, because there had been a boy at playgroup who took a plastic toy from me, but I was only three when I grabbed it back and smacked his bottom with it. I wished I could look at Mum without wondering whether really I was to blame, because I had called him over. I heard my voice, small in my head, calling his name, calling him 'Princess'.

"There is no question," said the head, "of Daisy hurting anyone. But she was there, a witness, and involved. Weren't you, Daisy?"

I liked him. It wasn't his fault and he was trying to be fair. His voice was deep but kind.

"Yes," I said.

Mum reached over and touched my hand.

"Tell us what happened, Daisy," said Mr Ogabe, and I tried, but the tears came throbbing back and getting in the way of the words. I knew I had to try to tell about the turnip with DW on its breasts, even though the evidence was on the roof. As it came out, slowly, detail by detail, I saw Mum's eyes widen with horror. I saw her begin to understand. She reached for my hand.

"This nickname," said Mr Ogabe, "has been used for a long time? Just by Kevin?"

"For a long time," I said. "Not just Kevin."

"And tell me about George."

I told him George had been kind when I had no friends. I told him George wanted to stop Kevin making me unhappy.

"Whose idea was it to cut Kevin's hair?"

I looked at him. I suppose I was asking him not to make me do this, not to George. I started to cry again. And then I knew, suddenly. There was a way out, and I took it. I ran headlong down it.

"Mine," I said. "I got the scissors. I gave them to George. It was my fault."

"Daisy ..." said Mum. I think even then she wondered, but she wasn't sure any more.

"But he did the cutting?"

"Only because I told him to."

Mr Ogabe remarked to Mum that George doing what he was told was something of a first and that clearly I had more authority over him than anyone else. I said nothing.

"So the plan was to give him a haircut," he said to me. "Your plan?"

I nodded.

"And the rest was an accident?"

"Yes. George never meant to hurt him."

"I see."

"So, Daisy, tell me, who is most to blame for this incident?" he pushed me, very quietly, the words falling heavily, leaving pauses in their wake. "Kevin, or George, or you?"

There was only one way to finish now I had started. And in that moment I thought I knew where everyone in Y6 would lay the blame, now that Kevin was in hospital. Kevin, who could get people laughing. Kevin with the pretty face.

"I am," I said.

Mum shook her head. Her hands fell on her lap as if she had dropped them by mistake. She had edged further off the front of the chair and her toes were balancing like a dancer.

"No, Daisy, you're not," she announced. "I am. I'm to blame for being so dense and naïve and wrapped up in my own problems that I didn't see, guess, work it out. Because this is systematic victimisation. Cruelty. This boy Kevin has bullied you for half a term, and you've taken it, quietly, sadly, bravely. The teachers have been blind to it, just like I have. The only one who has stood up for you and tried to make it better is this boy

119

George. And quite frankly, I'd like to shake his hand. Take him out to lunch! Give him a hug!"

I hadn't seen her quite like this before. She was what Flame would call awesome. Mr Ogabe's mouth was open to butt in but he never quite found the moment.

"Of course," she said, before he could, "I'm sorry that this Kevin is hurt, but that was never intended."

"No," said Mr Ogabe, "it seems not. George says not and I am inclined to believe him. In fact, Daisy, I am more inclined to believe him than you."

I stared.

"Where did the scissors come from?"

I tried to shape my mouth round a convincing possibility, but he stopped me before my brain could supply one.

"George was able to say exactly where he found them. And he told me that although you were there, watching, and in his words, horrified, you had no idea what he was planning to do and played no part in it at all."

Mum looked at me, her shoulders falling, and I realised how much I had been hurting her when I tried to protect George. But failed.

The interview was a long way from over. I had to give more examples of the bullying while Mr Ogabe made notes. Then I did the nodding while he told me that if I had only spoken to him or Mrs Young, or Mum, right at the start, none of the rest need have happened.

"I know what you were doing," murmured Mum. "You were being brave enough for two," and her voice was angry, but not with me. "Me and my big, stupid mouth."

Mr Ogabe suggested that Mum take me home for the rest of the day, but promised that he would let us know when the school heard from the hospital. He shook hands with Mum and told me it was true that I was a very brave girl, but that lying to try to save someone else wasn't brave. In a court it would be perjury. I hadn't thought of that. Mum didn't seem to like the word and as soon as we were out of the door and in the car park she said, "Perjury, my eye! It was heroism!" And then told me never to be that kind of hero again.

Kevin's cut needed seven stitches, but it wasn't what the hospital called serious. He would be back at school soon. I wondered whether his mum and dad were very angry with George, but Mr Ogabe didn't say. Mum wanted to know whether I'd like to move to a different school, but I said no, because of Mrs Young and the White Witch, and because I was the only friend Nina had. It was a long afternoon, cold and still and strange. It felt like an ending but I knew it wasn't and I was worried, for George and for Kevin too. In the end I slept in my clothes on the bed, and Mum put her own duvet over me. But when I woke up it still wasn't over.

I had to ask Mum to try to forget about it, all of it, and she said she wasn't sure she could. She'd rung Dad already, because he had to know. He drove over after work, even though I said he didn't need to, and even though I told them both I didn't want to talk about it any more.

They didn't make me. But they talked, a lot, and I played music so I didn't have to hear them. And I locked my diary. I couldn't face it any more.

Then Dad came to say goodbye. He pulled my head close to his chest and squeezed me tight.

"A whole week, Daise," he said. "We had a whole week but you never said a word. Were you afraid I'd deck this Kevin and land myself in jail?"

I didn't answer, although I could imagine it: a cartoon-style left hook from Dad and a flattened Kevin. It was funnier than real life, with less blood.

"Anyway," he said, "he's got what he deserved now."

I looked at him. He can be such a boy.

"That's not how it works," I told him. "Things happen, whether people deserve them or not."

He shook his head and I think it was at himself.

"Yeah," he said. "I know. I do know really. But goodies and baddies make it simpler. Just desserts and payback. You know the kind of thing." He smiled. "I'll grow up one day."

"Do you promise?" I said.

But he didn't, and I knew it was because of the broken ones he wished he'd kept. I wanted to tell him I didn't expect him to be perfect just because he was my dad. We wanted the same thing, really: to trust each other with the truth. But words like those weren't in Dad's vocabulary.

"Oh, Daise," he said, suddenly casual on the doorstep, "Uncle Will has asked me over this weekend. We might go to the footy. Do you want to come, or stay with Mum?"

I tried to make sure my face didn't fall. I like my cousins, but there are five of them and at that time two of them were still at a sticky, grizzly age. And I didn't know them that well, because Dad and Uncle Will were never that good at making arrangements. Mum complained that most of their texts and emails were about Tottenham.

I said, only more tactfully, that I'd pass on the big match and all the noise that went with the offer, on and off the pitch. I didn't mention Flame, because I didn't want Dad to think he was the one I looked forward to seeing at weekends.

Mum was quiet after he left, but not in a worrying way. I thought perhaps they'd stopped blaming each other. I hoped so. I was tired of blame.

"Will you stay with me this weekend then?" she asked.

I nodded, but then my mouth opened.

"Maybe Flame would like to come too," she said, and smiled.

Chapter Twelve

Flame came on the train. We met him at the station, bike in tow. I glimpsed him as the carriages slowed past, but I was excited even before I first saw the train's nose in the distance. The anticipation started as soon as dance class finished and I was changing out of my leotard. I could feel it in my breathing, high in my chest, and in my eyes as they searched. I had never imagined him coming to me. It was as if he belonged in London, and when he stepped out onto the platform all its smells and sounds and colours and flavours followed him.

His little brother was fair and fluffy, and wore dungarees under a duffel coat. He looked around seriously but silently through his glasses, which he pushed back up his nose as he examined me.

"Say hullo to Daisy, Blue," Flame told him.

He did, and I said hullo back. Mum was saying hi too, to the tall, thin lady who held on to Blue with one hand and a buggy with the other. His fluffiness came from her. A bush of sandy hair sprouted out behind her in a pony tail, but thick strands fell free over her face. She tucked one behind a small ear. Her eyebrows and eyelashes hadn't quite vanished like mine, but they were pale, and made her eyes look startling. But I liked her smile, which stretched wide. She wore narrow, long red jeans, a short denim jacket, and basketball-type trainers that were made from denim off-cuts as well as car tyres (Flame had told me about those).

"It's so nice of you to invite us," she told Mum, as they did the twin kisses lean, both cheeks each. "I'm Fliss."

"I'm glad you could come," said Mum, volunteering her own name, Molly.

Flame said I could ride his bike.

"Wait till you get down the steps!" cried Mum, as we rushed ahead while Blue climbed without complaining into his buggy. The next moment I heard from behind us an unexpected chortling sort of laugh that sounded as if it bounced around his throat on the way out. Flame shrugged with a kind of *Who knows?* grin on his face, but I could tell he was proud.

"Barking!" he called back at the buggy, and right on cue came yelps and woofs that stopped only to give way to more laughter.

Flame said that was game number eleven and I'd probably get to know them all. I'd never wished I had a little brother before, and I wondered, if I did, whether he'd be bald like me.

It started to rain, Noah's Ark style, as we approached the house and Flame and I waited under cover on the doorstep while the mothers ran for it. Blue laughed, punching and kicking at his capsule of plastic just to enjoy the watery thwacks on the inside as well as the needlepoint beating on the outside. I saw Tamsin's face at her bedroom window so I wasn't surprised when there was a knock at the door just as Mum had put the kettle on and handed Fliss a towel for her dripping hair.

Mum let Tamsin in. It wasn't that I wanted her to clear off, not exactly. I just wanted Flame to myself. She wore a very red lipstick and her hooped earrings were so big and thick they would almost make Blue a bike. Her hair had collected about seven drops of rain on the big stride across from her house to mine but she produced a brush from her handbag, asked for a hairdryer and seemed disappointed by the lack of attachments on ours. She knelt with the power on full in front of a mirror Mum fetched her, smiling every now and then. I decided the smiles were for Flame, not me.

"We could say anything," said Flame to me, "and she wouldn't hear. I could say she wouldn't make the short list for the Friend of the Year award and she'd just smile."

"She's sorry," I said. "She's used to me now."

"Has she said so?"

"Not exactly."

Flame didn't seem to think that was good enough but I changed the subject to polar bears because I'd been trying to work out how to restart my campaign. We talked about flyers and putting them through people's doors.

Flame reckoned they just get recycled or binned and we needed a whole new approach that would make everyone think.

"Let's ride around the town with placards round our necks saying GET ON YOUR BIKE on one side and FOR CLEANER AIR on the other," I said.

"All the cars will soak us! Their windscreens will be steamed up, the wipers will be on full and they won't even see us. And the words will get washed away."

I couldn't argue with that. Tamsin turned the noise off, checked her lips and wanted to know what she'd missed so I told her.

"You could steal everyone's remote, so no one could watch any telly," she said, and smiled cheekily. "But don't take mine."

Flame told her it was serious and she said, "Sorreeee," with a down mouth. "Polar bear cubs are sooooooo cute," she added, "but when they grow up they're a bit ... mean."

"So are some people," said Flame, "but they've still got the right to live."

"I'd rather save kittens," said Tamsin.

Flame had to explain that they are not an endangered species. Tamsin was plaiting a few strands of hair, quickly but meticulously, looking up at him for approval every few seconds, and I realised she was trying to copy him. For one private crackle of a moment I wondered whether she would be using the red tissue and sequins again soon, and I had to tell myself Flame would rather be with me. Wouldn't he?

Mum suggested we baked our own bread rolls for tea while we planned our campaign. Tamsin didn't like the colour, texture or smell of the yeast and wouldn't touch hers, so Flame handled it for her. And then at the dough stage she made a fuss about the stickiness caught in her fingernails. Blue was desperate to get his hands in the mixture, but she mouthed the word "Germs" as if he had more than his fair share. Blue repeated the word as if germs were happy little creatures and he hoped he'd find a crowd of them. When I saw Fliss signal with her palms and shoulders up and mouthe to Mum *"What planet is she from?"* I realised that for a change I wasn't the odd one out. Tamsin was, and she would have hated it if she'd known.

While the kitchen began to smell completely delicious we played Scrabble and Tamsin made SEXY on her holder and passed it to Flame with a big-eyed smile. I couldn't believe it. What were the chances of her getting those letters? And she scored a ridiculous number of points after Flame showed her a better place to put it. She thanked him and told him he was soooo clever. Then she wanted to stop once he'd told her she was in the lead now.

"You're not supposed to help other people," I told him.

"Don't see why not," he said, and Mum looked at me because it wasn't the kind of thing she expected me to say.

And then, as Tamsin insisted she'd won, and we cleared the letters away, I had my idea.

"A walk into town one Saturday!" I cried. "As many people as possible all leaving their cars behind. And we could dress up as polar bears and get the local paper to cover it, and show how quick it is."

"I've got white boots," said Tamsin, "but I'm not wearing them if it's messy weather."

"You could buy some white lipstick and eye shadow," said Fliss, and Tamsin didn't realise she was being teased and thought it was a cool idea.

Flame was high fiving me.

"Genius!"

Tamsin looked unimpressed. I thought maybe she was trying to find a reason why my idea was not so brilliant after all, and that explained her sudden quietness and the straightness of her red mouth. We looked at one of those fold-up maps you can never fold back again. There must be thousands of people like us living less than two miles from town, but most of them automatically jumped in their cars. But on LEG IT day we would ask them to walk, or cycle, and if they enjoyed it they might do it again.

Tamsin wanted to wait until the following summer because the weather was so horrible in November, but I said everyone would be too hot then to dress up as polar bears. Mum and Fliss made a list of people to call and we started making posters, taking turns to use the computer Mum had just bought but also using felt tips and paper collage.

"And we'll do one in Putney too," said Flame, "on the same day. We'll tell the press and the BBC and maybe other towns will organise their own."

"We'll need banners," said Mum. "I'm sure Liz could do with a break from wedding dresses."

We were all working at the kitchen table, apart from Blue who was playing his own soundtrack with pans and spoons. He'd arranged the contents of Mum's cupboard like a steel band. Now he wiggled his bottom and shoulders in between bashes.

Then the sun leaned in and touched us. We decided to leave everything for a practice LEG IT to the woods, straight away before darkness fell.

And I hoped, given her dislike for mud under her shoes and twigs in her hair, that Tamsin wouldn't come, but Fliss was encouraging her and she agreed as long as she could change first. I was glad when Kay came to the rescue and collected her, even though I could tell she didn't want to be dragged away from Flame. And I felt meaner than I'd ever felt before.

If I'm honest, though, I forgot her in the woods. First we saw the deer, a whole line of them, threading through our view like beads, one after another. When they stopped they were still as the trees, but alert, watching us as intently as we watched them. And then there was the Eeyore house we made together, with everyone helping, even Blue, one twig at a time. As it grew colder and the light faded, I wished it was summer and they could all stay later, but by seven they were on the train home and everything felt suddenly quiet, the fizz flat, the day's energy all used up.

We tidied up. Blue seemed to have rearranged every movable object in the house. Mum found a wooden spoon in the washing machine and dough clinging to doorways and chairs.

"Fliss makes me feel inadequate," she sighed. "I wish I had the guts to take a hammer to a war plane so it can't drop bombs on anyone."

Apparently Fliss did that when she was very young, and had to go on trial, but the judge found her and the older women innocent, because although they had committed one crime, they did it to prevent a much bigger crime against humanity. A lot of people were angry about the verdict and thought the judge had lost his senses. After all, it was criminal damage. The plane was out of action. They had broken in to the base and trespassed and cost the Ministry of Defence a lot of money. Fliss knew she had been lucky. She might have gone to prison, and she couldn't attempt anything so risky now because of Flame and Blue. Mum called her "magnificent" and decided she was "weedy" herself.

"Don't be silly," I said, and told her she was a great mum and a good artist and I loved her.

"I haven't been very big or brave," she said, "but you'll be glad to know the crying is going to stop. Fliss has made a new life since she split up with Kyle. A full life, not a little, selfish one. And so can I."

I smiled, but I wished I could make her believe she was fine just the way she was.

"We're all different," I said. "I should know."

She kissed the top of my head, and said it felt cold. I knew she kept an eye on it, in case a first hair decided to brave the winter air and push through, but I left that to her.

"I'd give it up, if I could," she said. "I'd do a deal. My hair for yours. I wish I could."

"I know," I said.

She pulled a little knitted cap down to my ears. I never realised how much heat the body loses through the scalp if it's not coated by nature. It isn't just for decoration. It's insulation and without it winter evenings chill you to your toes.

"I can see why you think the world of Flame," she told me. "Maybe you don't realise it, but he thinks the world of you too."

I didn't argue. She teased me for blushing but I wasn't. I was just warming through from the head down.

After that life had a new buzz. At school we were rehearsing and I was getting witchier by the day. Home was campaign headquarters. Liz and Mum made banners, the local paper ran an article saying that LEG IT was going to happen and the local radio station rang up wanting details. Mr Ogabe supported it and spoke about it in assembly, encouraging everyone to join in. He handed over to me to tell everyone about the polar bears and their disappearing habitat and I managed quite well. Mrs Young promised she'd take part and so did lots of the people in my class. It seemed to be turning into a competition about who could be the best polar bear and the charity shops were running out of white jumpers fast.

Kevin Price didn't say a word about polar bears, LEG IT or anything else to do with me. He was back at school with his stitches showing because the hair cut George had given him was so wild his mum had obviously decided the only thing to do was clear away the mess. So he had more hair than me, but not much. But although he looked fiercer, with his short spikes and his zigzag cut, he was quieter, and seemed to make a point of looking beyond me or past me. I couldn't tell whether he hated me, or was acting on strict orders from his parents and the school. Or both. Or whether there was any chance Mum was right and he'd learned some kind of lesson. I just enjoyed feeling bigger and stronger and not having to work at being unafraid.

George still hadn't come back and there were rumours that he'd been expelled but when Mum checked with Mr Ogabe he said that wasn't true. He hoped George would be back soon. I wanted to write him a letter so Mum got the address from the school secretary, but then I held the pen in the air after *Dear George* and couldn't think what to say. In the end I just said I missed him and told him about LEG IT, said he'd make a great polar bear and then worried, when I'd posted it, that he might take offence. He didn't reply. Every day I looked out for him in the playground but he never appeared.

LEG IT Saturday was a great day but when I woke my first thought was that Flame would be in Putney, because thanks to our publicity a few other communities were doing the same thing at the same time. I wished we could have been polar bears together. Kyle, Fliss and Blue and Flame's stepdad Ian all took part. My dad was supposed to join them but had some work that was running late and didn't show. At my end there was Mum, Auntie Sue and Uncle Ben, both my teenage cousins and some of their friends, all smiling much more than usual, plus Liz and her soon-to-be husband, plus Matthew the choirmaster with a couple of older women from Mum's church, and Kay and Tamsin. Along with about two hundred others. And we looked amazing, even though Tamsin slowed us down because of the heels on her white boots. We were a bright white snaking chain of rhythm heading into town, with people joining from the houses we passed and others waving from windows.

I kept the local paper's report, so here is what they printed, under the headline LOCALS LEG IT FOR POLAR BEARS, with a photograph of white bodies along the high street:

More than three hundred people took part in Saturday's LEG IT into town, most of them dressed in white from top to toe to draw attention to the plight of polar bears losing their habitat due to global warming. The walk, which was also a cycle ride, was to encourage more of us to leave our cars behind when we go into town and reduce our carbon footprints.

The campaign was masterminded by young environmental activist Daisy Waterhouse, age 11. Daisy was delighted that the same kind of event was happening in other communities.

"If we all think a bit more and try a bit harder," said Daisy, "we can make a difference. It isn't just about polar bears. It's about the earth."

Daisy's mother, pictured with her above, said she was very proud. "But it's not a one off," said Molly Waterhouse, who works at The Art House. "This is about changing the way we live."

Mum was pleased they got the quotes right, but she had also been quite angry, because a reporter had rung to ask whether I'd had chemotherapy. He'd been disappointed to hear it was only alopecia, but then had called back for more details and wanted a photo of me without my fluffy white hat. Mum put the phone down on him before she said something rude that broke her own rules.

I'd hoped George might join in the procession, and looked out for a polar bear the right shape and size with that cowboy walk of his, but I didn't see him. People at school were starting to say he'd left and I heard Kevin say, one day in the cloakroom, that he was locked up in a place for criminals who were too young to go to jail. I knew it couldn't be right. I just wondered what made Kevin say it, apart from wishful thinking. I supposed the strain of not saying or doing anything horrible was bound to tell eventually. He must have been tightly packed inside with stored-up hostility, like a grenade ready to explode with maximum damage.

He didn't know I'd overheard. I stepped on to the shoe racks and put my head over the top to let him see me.

"That's not true," I said, loudly enough for everyone in the cloakroom to hear.

"Yeah?" he said, but not very loudly. "What do you know about it?"

"I know," I said, "that sometimes the judge can see that small crimes are committed to prevent bigger crimes." I didn't add the phrase *against humanity* because that seemed a bit over the top for Kevin Price. And I wasn't sure he'd know the meaning of the word.

He knotted his forehead so tightly that I could see it hurt where the stitches were. He winced, his teeth set. He didn't understand and for a long moment I could see he didn't like having nothing to say, especially to me.

"Sorry," he said eventually, "I didn't realise we had a local celebrity in the cloakroom. I'd have asked for your autograph if I'd known."

Yaz did laugh; it's a kind of reflex with him when Kevin speaks, like a nervous tic. But one of the Y1 children took the hint and produced the back of a school newsletter for me to sign my name. Then a few more copied, gathering around expectantly. Kevin was gone rather quickly.

"Yo!" said Flame, when I told him on the phone, and whooped like someone at a concert wanting an extra song. Even on the other end of the phone he could tell that I was smiling, and I was glad he couldn't see me, because I wanted to smile too. I just wasn't sure I could.

Chapter Thirteen

I hadn't seen Dad for a while. He sent texts as if he thought each word cost a pound, messages like *All right Twinkletoes?* and *How's White Witch doing?* and *Saved world yet?* but I always liked getting them. Mum said she didn't want him to feel jealous, because she'd got me, and I'd got Flame. She said he wasn't always as chirpy on the inside as he was on the outside, but I knew that already.

The next weekend I asked him if he'd got a new girlfriend and he said he'd decided to be picky.

"Good," I said. Then I grinned. "But you might be in trouble if the women out there are doing the same."

"Oy!" he protested, and chased me round the kitchen with a recipe book to whack me with. "What about my natural charm and sense of humour? What about my lovely hair?"

He let the book fall from the air, where it was poised over my cotton-coated scalp. He thudded it down on the worktop and slapped his palm to his forehead.

"Oh, Daise! I'm sorry. Gaffe of the day."

I told him not to be silly. He did have nice hair. I'd always wished mine had been more like his, less hay and more silk.

"It'll grow back soon. Any day," he said, but I stopped him peering because I wasn't like a flower pot on a window sill. Each day didn't bring more green, more stretch and reach.

"You don't know," I told him. "You shouldn't make promises you can't keep. It might never grow. I might be like this for ever."

He pulled me to him. I was growing fast but I still tucked under his arm.

"Not a promise, Daise. A hope. A wish."

"I don't want to hope," I said. "Then I won't be disappointed."

My voice was calm. It didn't wobble. Dad was the one who seemed upset, so upset that he couldn't seem to find a joke. Or even a gaffe.

"Anyway," I said, "there must be a planet somewhere full of people with bald heads who shave off any disgusting hair that tries to make them look freaky. If there is, I'm going to live there."

"Don't," he said. "I'd have to come too or I'd miss you too much."

"They'd stare at you," I said. "They'd mutter and point and call you names."

"I'd survive," said Dad, and launched into the song, with disco dance moves like fingers pointing to the corners of the room. He was too busy singing to hear me when I said I'd survive too.

But I wondered, as he watched the football results and didn't notice me watching him, whether he meant it about missing me, because I think some dads are meant to be part-time. They just have too many other details in their heads.

Flame arrived that night but I must have been asleep by then. I found a note through the door: *Will knock for you at half past seven. F.* It was nearly seven by the time I unfolded it sleepily, so I woke Dad, who didn't seem too pleased once he discovered there was no fire.

"Why so early?" he yawned, eyebrows stretching and meeting again.

"Everyone knows this is the best time," I told him.

"Yes, for sleeping soundly!" he cried.

"No, for seeing things!" I shouted at the sprouting head peeking out under the duvet.

But I had no idea, none. If I'd imagined for a moment what we would be seeing, I would have dragged him out of bed by the legs. Soaked a flannel in ice cold water. Roared into his ears.

Flame and Kyle were on time. They always seemed as if their power was on full, their batteries new. Dad didn't have much to say for himself once he finally appeared, apart from grunting "All right?" a few times as if he was talking in his sleep.

The night still hung around as we stepped outside, but as we walked it drifted away, letting through the thinnest of morning light. Putney was very pale and not much more wide awake than Dad. The air was thick with clinging winter, damp on my clothes but sharp inside my mouth. It burned my ears where they peeped out under my wool hat. At first we didn't speak much. Each stride was enough effort, and we set off at a pace.

On the bridge Flame and I ran ahead. He told me how great it had been when a long white line of bears had crossed it, almost from one end to the other. But now it was only us. We looked down at the iron-grey water, its glint dim and cold. Flame handed me some autumn leaves he had collected. Some of them were crinkle-dry and faded now, but in the November light they seemed like a riot of bonfire colour. We dropped them one at a time to watch them float, like living things with their own twist and turn and place to go.

Runners began to appear, some light, lean and long-legged and some sagging to a sweaty shuffle. Like us they were heading past the Star and Garter and Putney pier, towards the trees and the boat houses. The two of us began to power walk in time, like Roman soldiers, the rhythm of our feet just one beat. There was a moment when my head was so close to Flame's that when I watched our breath misting ahead of us I thought it might merge in one cloud.

In one boat house a crew in fleeces were easing a boat free. A pair of rowers sat busily in the water, oars askew, almost ready, while Canadian geese, seagulls and ducks bobbed close by. Flame named the trees. I repeated them, and we incorporated them into our marching instead of Hup two three four. Poplar. Poplar. Horse chestnut. Horse chestnut. Lime. Lime. We had left the blue railings behind now and were on the wide raised path that shelved down to scree. Then we found our favourite willow, twisted and reaching like a jungle gym, reaching out and down and around just asking to be climbed. Flame detached a soggy plastic bag caught from one branch, shaking the wetness from it

135

and zipping it in his pocket. We dangled and swung and balanced while Kyle tried to teach Dad Tai Chi. It wasn't as funny as we made out, but Flame laughed so much he pretended he nearly fell from the tree.

Fulham F.C. was white and lit up on the other side of the river and Dad was talking football now. Flame jumped down onto the dark brown stones that made a kind of empty beach, his trainers sinking with a rattle. I followed, unsteady but soon overtaking.

"Don't go too close to the water," called Dad.

"We're swimming!" I told him. "Haven't you got your trunks?"

"No, man, skinny dipping!" said Kyle. "Didn't Flame say?"

"Ho ho," muttered Dad, between teeth that were trying not to chatter.

There was a straggling boat house with no sign of life. The dads sat down on its slipway, and I heard words like 'Ashes' and 'Flintoff' so I knew they'd moved on to cricket. The slope wasn't really that steep but I pretended it was a climbing wall and we stretched our way up it, from one wooden runner to another, with a dramatic commentary. Then, at the top, we looked at each other, grinned, chorused "Go!" and ran down it, skimming over the ridges and opening our mouths to let the loudness out, until we staggered into scree again.

We wouldn't have made so much noise if we'd known. We would have whispered, hardly daring to place our feet for the scrunch and squelch. I saw it first, more a wave than a shape, too much movement for wind, and Flame saw it on my face, my opening mouth and snatched gaze. He lifted a spread hand to the dads. Kyle stopped mid-sentence. A dull gleam of a mound butted out of the water and down again. No mistake this time. No wishful thinking. It was alive and enormous and it was swimming, closer to us than the football club, ploughing a tug on the water.

"It's not, is it?" asked Dad.

Kyle produced binoculars from his pocket. He followed the creature with them, saying nothing, then passed them to Flame, who watched, then gave them to me. I took a moment to train them on the right stretch of steely water. But when I did I almost lifted both feet from the stones.

"The head?" asked Kyle, as I focused the binoculars. They were looking to me for words and I wanted them to be right. I was thinking hippo, but not quite. The creature was all head, hull-shaped, knobbly and mottled grey.

A noise broke the silence of my thinking. It was whale song, but it didn't sound like the kind of soothing CD Auntie Sue bought in a pack of two along with watery music of the rainforest. It sounded raw and wild and wrong.

"It's in trouble," said Kyle, and he was producing a mobile. "It needs help."

Though we hadn't moved, the whale seemed closer now. It wasn't making progress. It was floundering. It couldn't swim.

"This one's not gonna die," said Flame, his teeth clenched tight.

We heard Kyle talking into the phone, agitated now he had to listen, saying, "Yeah, man. Sure."

"Jamie," said Flame. "He's a marine mammal medic who works with the B.D.M.L.R.. Those guys know what they're doing."

I didn't know what the initials stood for but I knew a whole team of experts had tried to save that other whale, the bottlenose, because I'd seen the news, got angry at the stupid names in the papers like 'Celebrity Big Blubber' and 'Gonzo', and cried when it died. I was afraid this whale would die. It was too slow and it wasn't powering. It was hardly even gliding but drifting now, like wood caught up and down on the tide.

"The water isn't deep enough, is it?" I asked.

"It's used to seven hundred metres," said Flame. "The river's no more than five."

I had no idea. I imagined its panic. I heard it in another burst of song. Flame had the binoculars now but he let Dad have a look. And Dad swore.

"The size of it!" he gasped. "What the hell is it doing here?"

"Just took a wrong turn, maybe," said Kyle. "Pollution can disorient them. So can military sonar, when they're testing. And

137

when they're not well, they can lose their bearings, same way we get dizzy or fuzzy with flu."

He was texting now. A pair of cyclists in helmets raced past, too focused on the path ahead to notice the water, but a man with a dog had stopped behind us to stare.

"Am I hallucinating?" he called.

"Wish you were," said Kyle.

The dog, which was black and frisky, didn't care and wouldn't be stopped, so the man said he'd check on progress on his way back later. We knew there would be a crowd before long. It was Flame who saw the fibre glass scull, its long thin nose starting to break into the frame of our vision, the frame we were glued to like a widescreen, with the whale at the centre of it. It was just a rowing boat, no engine to traumatise, no propeller to rip flesh, but it was spearing too fast towards us, and we couldn't let it get any closer. So we ran, the four of us, even Dad, waving our arms like windmills, like Bobbie in *The Railway Children* trying to stop the train, but without red petticoats. Maybe they saw the whale, or maybe they didn't, but they stopped and let their oars rest. And slowly they manoeuvred that needle of a boat around, backtracking slowly. It was skill.

Joggers are obsessive. Some of them don't stop even for whales lost in the Thames. Others did. Some people didn't mind showing their ignorance. Others had opinions. But Flame knew.

"Sperm whale," he said. "Could be twenty metres long. Twice the size of a bottlenose. It's not curvy like a dolphin. More of a log."

And suddenly it came back to me, my pop-up whale book with tabs to pull and folds to open. The sperm whale. Not pretty at all, so Tamsin wouldn't like it. I could see in my head the picture of it nose-diving, jaw open, a giant squid with a leafy snout and tentacles like a cat-of-nine-tails whip about to be swallowed.

"It can dive deeper than any other whale," I said, "for food."

But I knew it wouldn't find any salmon-pink squid hanging around in the Thames the way the picture had hung in the bottom corner of the page since I was three. When you folded the page back, the jaws of the whale closed in on all those arms, one half deep and hippo-like, the other spearing up like a giant saw.

Flame shot me a smile, but it didn't last because we both knew there might not be enough food in the river for this whale, and that it had no room to dive. It was like a real duck, not a rubber one, trying to swim in a baby bath. This time, if someone didn't do something soon, the victim wasn't going to be the squid but the whale.

I shivered suddenly, because I'd forgotten how cold I was but my body hadn't. Kyle had been watching through the binoculars for a while. He told us he was sure now it was a baby.

"Separated from its mother and the rest of the females. That's unusual. They stay close."

If Tamsin heard that, she'd call it cute after all. But it wasn't a children's animation and I wasn't confident there would be a happy ending. And I realised then that what was happening was awesome and amazing and the biggest thrill of my entire life, but also terrible. Miserable. And I wished I wasn't there, even though I knew I'd never forget that I was, however long I lived.

Dad edged down to me and muttered that he was afraid I'd catch cold and Mum would be furious. He knew I wouldn't be going anywhere, so he said he'd hurry back to the flat for scarves, gloves, flasks of hot chocolate and soya bacon doorsteps.

Kyle's friend Jamie didn't take long. He brought a young woman with a Chinese name who said we could call her Tintin like her relatives back home. She had very small features but her eyelashes were thick and black. Jamie and Tintin had cameras as well as binoculars and agreed with everything Flame and Kyle had decided.

"Its mother will be frantic," said Tintin. "The females stay together in little groups, nursing their young till they are about three years old."

The whale, however huge, was a toddler. It was hard to imagine a mother four or five times its size and weight. But

Jamie said that a sperm whale did get stranded in the Humber estuary not so long ago.

"And a dead male was washed up on a beach in Oregon back in 1970. People came to stare and take photos in front of it for a while but then the transport department wanted to get rid of it." He paused. "They filled it with half a ton of dynamite. And you don't want to know the rest."

My hands covered my mouth. He was right. I didn't. I was sure there were lots of facts my pop-up book hadn't told me about sperm whales but I didn't really want to know them either. What I wanted to know was what could be done. I wanted to know why we weren't in the water now.

"How will you save her?" asked Flame.

Jamie and Tintin looked at each other and I didn't like the silence they were sharing.

"I know it went wrong with that bottlenose but it was bleeding, wasn't it?" I cried. "This one isn't, is it? So if it's only stranded..."

"Don't worry," said Kyle. "The B.D.M.L.R. will do everything they can." And Jamie agreed. Flame must have guessed I hadn't worked the initials out so he told me: British Divers Marine Life Rescue. I was glad to hear the final word. But when Dad returned with everything he'd promised they still hadn't arrived, although the group of early rising members of the public was slowly growing into quite a gathering. Dad said he'd seen a BBC van, parked up near the old pub.

That was when everything started to move on to another level, from a small crowd of dog walkers to a TV crew and, almost at the same time, the team from the B.D.M.L.R., who had a huge van too, full of equipment that I supposed they planned to use to help the whale.

I called Mum and told her to watch the news. Flame and I got blocked by bigger bodies but we didn't care about that. We were hardly going to wave and grin our way into people's living rooms.

The reporter asked the experts on camera what they were going to do and they used the word 'monitor'. I knew it meant they would keep an eye on the situation, a close eye, but it didn't seem enough. An eye was not as much use as a rescue. Maybe I looked really agitated, or maybe the guy with the microphone just remembered that I had been the first one to spot the whale, but he turned to me, checked my name on his notes before he introduced me, and wanted to know how I'd felt.

"Amazed," I said. "Excited. But now I'm just worried."

"This is Tim Granby from Putney, where everyone shares Daisy's concern. It may be early for most of us, but for the sperm whale in the Thames, time could be running out."

As the broadcast finished I felt such a wild, desperate helplessness that I wanted to beat the smile off the face of Tim Granby, who seemed to care more about how his piece had gone than how the whale might be doing. He went to get coffee and the rest of us just watched and talked. It was still before nine in the morning but I felt really tired just wondering how exhausted that baby whale must be, just trying to keep afloat, and searching for its mother in a strange, shallow world.

I knew some of the people who had watched on TV would be heading our way. I didn't blame them; I'd do the same. But I was beginning to feel lost in the crowd myself. I didn't expect the monitoring to change quite so quickly into action.

The whale was barely moving. Jamie used the word 'beached'. The tide was still very much out, but there was deeper water further out past Fulham, and if the calf was too confused to find it herself we would have to give her a nudge. Divers emerged in red wetsuits. Jamie and Tintin put on yellow lifejackets. Dad didn't want me to go, until he saw my eyes. He had brought wellies back with him, but they weren't really up to the job. It was a matter of wading in.

"No kids," said Bruce, who seemed to be in charge.

"We'll look after them," said Kyle. "They're strong swimmers."

"So was the whale," said Bruce.

Dad would have let me climb on his shoulders, piggyback, higher in the water, until he realised he'd probably just topple backwards with the weight of me. Unlike the whale, I wasn't a toddler any more. Flame wanted to make a human chain leading into the water. But in the end it was the adults, including a few passers-by, who started to heave their way in. I knew the water must be freezing. I knew Mum wouldn't want me in there. But it seemed so hard, when we had found it, that all we could do was watch from the shore.

Dad stayed with us. Kyle joined in. Through the binoculars we tried to see what he saw, up close. About twenty adults gathered round and tried not so much to push as guide, encourage. We heard them talking to it, coaxing, like parents trying to persuade a little child to eat his vegetables. Someone tried to mimic whale song rather unconvincingly.

Of course even a baby whale is powerful enough to break a boat or a limb. Jamie and Bruce made sure no one tried to touch so no one could report on the texture of the knobbles that were supposed to remind human beings of prunes. Flame and I listened, tried to hear through the helicopter above and the film crews shooting behind, tried to identify words that would be clues. And we saw the whale, which had been doing no more than drifting downstream with the ebb and upstream with the flow, make its move. The people cleared. The great body surged forward and out into the deepest water. Gathering speed, it seemed with sudden purpose to know where it was going. Of course we ran, Flame and I, along the path, our hearts racing as we tried to keep up the pace. But though we kept our eyes to the right, across the water, trying to hold it in view, our breathlessness only hurt in the cold air as we folded to a stop, the whale out of sight now, the binoculars beating uselessly against Flame's stomach.

"Daisy!"

Dad was running too, but not for long. He was out of condition, blowing out, arms across his chest.

"Enough now," he breathed, a big gulp of air between words. "She's free."

I was glad. We both were. It was great to see her swim. But we didn't celebrate. Our hands hung by our sides. It seemed like the beginning of the journey, not the destination. She had so far to go.

"Good luck, Katya," murmured Flame.

I thought he had chosen her a Russian name, but he meant Cacha, as in cachalot, which is another name for the sperm whale. The common cachalot. Only nothing we had seen that day felt common at all. It felt misty and unreal, and stretched tight with hope and fear.

"Will she make it," I asked, "all the way to the sea?"

"Maybe the others will find her," said Flame. "They'll hear and call and she'll follow their song to safety."

"The authorities must stop the ships!" I cried. "All of them! She could be hit by a propeller and bleed to death. Especially in darkness."

Dad told me not to get hysterical. I told him I wasn't. I was considering likelihood and outcomes. The wet people who had been in the water with the whale were struggling onto land and the B.D.M.L.R. were moving into action of a different kind.

"They'll follow at a safe distance," Kyle told us, "in case she needs more help."

He told us about large nets, lifting barges and pontoons like the two that had been used to move the bottlenose. But what they were using now was an inflatable boat with a rigid hull. My eyes must have asked but I knew it was useless.

"Home before we collapse from hypothermia," Dad told me, and Kyle agreed. His hair was dripping and he looked ragged, skin tight around his cheekbones, his eyes raw. Someone threw a blanket over him.

Flame turned back to glance down the river. Nothing to see in the water. Just disturbance on land, streams of people, commentary in the air.

"Go, girl," he muttered, hands in fists, shaking without shivers.

We smiled, but the smiles were faint. It was hard to feel anything now, in the numbing winter air. Especially hope.

"Go, girl," I said.

Chapter Fourteen

We didn't know what to do with ourselves. Not once we'd showered, clutched steaming mugs of hot chocolate close to our faces, and spent ages channel-hopping to find TV coverage of Katya. Nothing seemed to matter as much as whatever might be happening miles away from us. Time felt like a gap. Empty, but full of worry. Kyle was calling Flame on Dad's house phone every five minutes but there was never anything much to report, and Dad said he was getting fed up with the two of us moping around like dishrags.

"Cheer up," he said. "Christmas is coming. Shall we go and get a tree?"

I stared. It was the middle of November. I said it would spoil it if we started so soon. Besides, it would be a strange Christmas. Who would I eat my dinner with?

"We'll have to sort that out," said Dad.

"My parents spend Christmas Day together," said Flame, "with my stepdad and his kids and his ex. And my cousins too. It's a party."

Dad and I looked at each other. That didn't sound like our family. Even my grandparents didn't really like to be in the same room any more.

I think Dad decided he didn't really want to be in the same room as the two of us any more, either, so he dragged us off to some big furniture place to buy a proper dining table and chairs. Of course we weren't very interested, until he said we could drive along by the river as much as possible and keep a look out for Katya, if that would make us less like wet lettuces and more like the red hot livewires he'd come to expect. We promised, but once we'd stared out of the car window for a few miles, peering across the dark grey water but seeing nothing but the rain teeming down the glass, I think we became rather limp and watery again, more Cos than Iceberg, even though it was cold enough.

"Eye? The London kind?" said Dad at the DIY checkout, surrounded by flatpacks. "You've been on at me for ages. It'll be quiet today. No queues."

I must have stared again.

"Because it's still raining," I said.

"We could go in the Aquarium too," said Dad, "if you want water without getting wet."

"Ah!" said Flame, and he was livewire again. "They're both on the river."

"Ever heard the word 'obsession'?" asked Dad.

"Ever heard the word 'magnificent' put in front of it?" I grinned, because if our whale wasn't a magnificent obsession I didn't know what was.

But then we had a long debate in the car, once we had squeezed in around the flatpacks, about how we would get along the river. Dad wanted to go by boat. I didn't want Katya cut to ribbons by its propellers, or even concussed by its hull. Dad said if anyone came off worse from a collision like that it would be the boat.

Flame rang to consult Kyle, who said the whale was last seen close to Battersea. Bikes seemed best, so we tented ourselves in plastic and headed out into the downpour. Dad kept using words like 'deranged', 'crazy' and just plain 'mad'. And 'pneumonia'.

We did see quite a lot more than we could have made out through car windows, but we didn't see the whale. And the river wasn't lined with lunatics like us, soaked to the skin in the hope of a sighting, because the weather seemed to have driven most of them home. We took what seemed like hours to get to the South Bank and the London Eye. I might have begged to give up half way if Flame hadn't been crouched down over the handlebars ahead of me as if it was an Olympic event with a gold medal at stake. But I wasn't in the best position to beg once my teeth got iced together, clamped tight and solid.

145

As the rain hadn't eased at all, we thought we'd try the Aquarium first. Dad said there would be sharks.

"Come on," he said. "Twenty-four hours ago sharks would have been exciting. Cool. Don't let a sperm whale spoil you for life."

It was a point, and the Aquarium was really good. We gave off some steam, and warmed through. The place was busy, but there wasn't much noise, as if beating a way through rain had worn everyone out. Dad said watching fish is soothing to the nerves. I think his nerves needed soothing. We saw sharks, but they were the small, curvy kind that looked like strange punctuation marks. No Great Whites. Still, I like the way they move, as if they're made of liquid themselves. Dad was distracted, looking around at a couple of whispering young women with hair that had frizzed out of the rain. He said he'd seen a film where a man meets someone beautiful at the Aquarium.

"Behave," I said. "Keep your eyes on the fish."

I liked the sideways walking crabs better than Dad's impression of them. And the sea horses were special, some grey, some brown, some almost black, but all beautiful in their fantasy way. After hot drinks we decided the weather wasn't going to improve by magic and it was now or never for the Eye. Dad had to make the decision into a joke.

"Eye? Eye?" he asked, looking from Flame to me.

I think he was waiting for one of us to play along and say "Captain." But we agreed with two okays, even though it was hard to leap with excitement. We weren't quite the only people at the foot of the giant wheel, but some of the tourists were bright and dry under large umbrellas. We were the only ones who had got wet enough between the Aquarium and the Eye to be mistaken for drowned rats dragged out of the river.

Dad wasn't in the best of moods by this time, but then he did that thing he does where he flicks a switch from miserable bear with a sore head to TV presenter overacting his excitement for the camera. It's called pretending to be having fun so children have half a chance of having fun themselves.

"Visibility will be poor today," said the guy taking the money. He said it slowly, like a sigh, as if we were a bit slow on the uptake.

"We'll suffer!" chirped Dad. "We're British. We're good at it."

"That's stupid," I said, because I'd seen places on *The News* where people starved, or feared for their lives.

Dad had been right about me wanting to go up on the London Eye for years, but the conditions weren't exactly the ones I'd had in mind.

"It'll be all grey and soupy," I said, "with streaks!"

Dad had already handed over the cash. Soup with streaks it was, then. In we got and up it went, eventually. We had to take the commentary's word for it that everything named was what it claimed to be. It was all a bit of a blur. And after a while I looked at Flame and saw that he was doing the same as me, resting his eyes down on the dark water down in the river rather than the thin, pale water drizzling steamily across the view.

On the embankment a quilted toddler below us spun helplessly. She was reaching out padded arms into the space where her family should be, finding it big and empty. We saw her mouth open wide in a silent stretch of a howl. Everyone nearby turned and watched, but no one moved. Then a wet woman with a baby in one of those carriers that tie to the chest broke away from a stall and ran to her, so that the baby's legs swung as if they were stuffed with rags.

"Do you think that's how Katya feels?" I asked Flame.

He nodded. His hood dripped.

"Helpless," he said. "Separated from a parent. Lost."

"Maybe not any more," I said, watching the mother crouch down to kiss the girl and stroke her hair. Then she grabbed her hand and they hurried across to a café for shelter.

Given the torrential sheets lashing the whole of London we weren't sure what to do about getting home, but after we'd waited some time for things to improve we collected our bikes and set off anyway. And that was how it happened.

Kyle texted Dad as we left the Eye. I don't think he wanted to tell us.

"It's your whale," Dad told us. "She's stranded again. Just down river from here. I suppose watching on TV isn't an option? A nice, cosy, warm, dry option?"

We both shook our heads. Dad said he thought not, and told me not to get upset. I didn't answer. How could I?

It wasn't far and there were plenty of clues to follow. As we approached the place, everything got thicker and louder and the air felt tight in spite of the rain. The film crews were there, and the B.D.M.L.R. plus Kyle, and everybody else, really. One of Mum's favourite film stars had turned up, but looked smaller in real life. And someone said the Mayor of London was there too, but it was hard to recognise anyone except Kyle under their hoods or umbrellas. Kyle stood out because he wasn't wearing anything on his head except his mass of hair, which looked flat now but must have been very, very heavy.

Katya herself was easy enough to find, because she was beached on the foreshore, very little of her in contact with the water at all. If the sun had been out we would have needed watering cans, dozens of them. But as it was, the rain was keeping her moist. Keeping her alive. For the first time, everyone could see the size and shape of her. I noticed her blowhole, very close to the front of her giant head, and saw that she had no dorsal fin, just ridges on her back that were rather like the runners on the slipways where Flame and I played. Her fluke was triangular, and very thick, way bigger than an elephant's ear.

Kyle was making his way towards us. He looked tired as well as wet. He pulled Flame towards him for an under the elbow hug, and gave me a warm smile, even though his mouth wouldn't open as wide as usual. Dad got a raised palm and a nod, and nodded back.

"She's not breathing so well," Kyle said. "Eight breaths per minute. Should be a lot more."

Jamie and Tintin were among the group around the whale. They were putting something around her blowhole. Kyle said it was lubricating gel, to ease the breathing.

"You were lucky to get in," he told us, nodding to the police who seemed to be multiplying. "They're enforcing an exclusion zone."

"She's not going to make it, is she?" I asked.

"She's distressed," he told me, quietly. "It's not looking so good."

"But can't they lift her and put her on a barge, and take her right out to Kent or somewhere?" asked Flame. "Maybe all she needs is deep water and she'll revive, get her strength back."

People were giving orders. We were told to turn mobiles off. The helicopter above must have been given orders to move away and its stuttery whine started to fade as it sideswung out of the frame and gathered height.

Tintin appeared at Kyle's shoulder and said that if we wanted to stay we'd have to stick with their team and keep a low profile, heads down. We nodded. Jamie was taking blood from Katya and conferring with the others. And all the time, as I watched, trying to see, trying to understand, the rain needled down. The wind whipped the plastic of my hood and flapped it noisily. But everything seemed slow and strangely still.

I heard someone say Shivering Sands and I knew it must be a place some way from where we were. The whale lay in rock and litter-strewn pebbled scree, no sand in sight. It sounded like a name from a story, a story with a happy ending. A fantasy.

"They're going to try to lift her," said Kyle, "and take her to the sea. Just off the coast of Margate."

"How long will it take?" I asked, stupidly, because who knew how long it would take just to move her, to haul her off the pebbles and on to the barge.

He shrugged.

"It'll take time."

"Will she survive?" I whispered, but it wasn't a question because there was no answer, not yet.

I suddenly realised how dark it was: not just the darkness of the winter and the rain but of dusk, of evening setting in. Mum would be expecting me home, and Dad couldn't call her now that mobiles were banned. I felt something cold and wet close around my hand. It was Flame's.

"If this was a story," I said, "all the whales in the North Sea would gather in a leaping mass, singing, and she'd follow."

"If it was a film, she'd jump over something," said Flame. "All our heads and the Thames Barrier too."

But there would be stars and music, I thought, and moonlight. Not hard rain that keeps on battering as if it's never going to stop. I looked at the whale. No amount of make-up would make her look good on camera, but I wished I could take a picture of her anyway, not the kind that would appear in the papers but mine, close up, no crowd.

In my mind I was beside her, the two of us, my head close to hers, talking to her, breathing into her, eye to eye, but there were no words I could have said that wouldn't sound empty as echoes.

In the real world, the loud, grey, wet world around me, stirred and urgent, things were starting to happen. A crane was being lowered in. I didn't even see it until a great rumble of creaking and groaning announced that it had arrived. Either a crane or a dinosaur, which couldn't have been too much heavier and which might have moved more freely, with fewer jolts and angles. Dad and Kyle wanted us further away. From quite a distance now we watched the lifting straps being passed under the whale as the B.D.M.L.R. and other people in yellow life jackets bobbed around Katya, all busy, all calling out, all part of a dripping plastic huddle that never stood still.

And there she went. It took so long I thought I'd lost all feeling in my toes. But there she went, up and into the barge. Not quite in one smooth move, but safely. And though she didn't fit, she rested across, head over the edge at one end, covered with a number of wet tarpaulins.

All other shipping had been called off until she was through. I knew because I checked. Everything that normally moved between this point on the river and Shivering Sands off the coast of Margate had stopped, and lay still. As still as the whale on the barge.

I didn't know what was taking so long. I kept asking, but people were running out of answers to give me. There was plenty of talk, but what about action? Surely Katya couldn't afford to hang around? Flame kept asking Kyle but he told us to leave it to the professionals.

"They know what they're doing," he said, in a voice that wanted us to leave it. "Trust them."

"Is there room for us?" cried Flame, in that voice of his that was so bright with excitement it was usually hard for his dad to resist, but we knew. We both knew. Then Kyle was talking to Jamie and we were climbing into the inflatable with some of the yellow lifejacket people, and the two dads were forcing the same jackets on us, fat and enormous and smelling strange. I felt as if I'd tip flat onto my face if anyone pushed me, but bounce straight back up again. But more than anything I felt nervous, and thrilled too, because I knew what it meant.

And eventually the signal came. Just a raised hand from Bruce, and the barge edged away, slowly, with human scaffolding gathered around the whale as if any feeble body could do anything at all to prop her up if she slid. Our boat did not get too close. We kept a distance, near enough to help but not to distract. We were moving too, equally slowly, the engine's throb lower and quieter than usual, as if a rein was pulled tight.

I did think of Mum, and what she would say if she knew where I was, among the yellow plastic officials, tucked away and highly unofficial, but part of the rescue team following a whale down the river. I was watching Katya every second, her fluke restless but her bulk motionless. I was willing her to be patient, to be brave, to save her strength and relax. But I wasn't managing much patience or relaxation myself.

"Whatcha thinking, Daise?"

It was Dad. I told him I'd been thinking about Mum.

"Me too," he said, in a soft, sad sort of voice.

"She's missing out," I said. "I wish she was here."

"You'll tell her," he said. "You're great with words. Better than I'll ever be."

I practised in my head. Words to describe the whale, the weather and the feelings. We used to do the special things together, all three of us.

"Moon, look!" said Flame, and there it was, thin through clouds, the darkness thickening from grey to black. London was lit up. No one had told the city that it was too early to start Christmas. The surface of the river flickered with reds and blues but the rain broke the patterns into fragments. We looked for stars to name but the sky was as bedraggled as we were. Visibility poor all round.

As we moved downstream the moon did peer through now and then, not whole or bright but not completely lost. It made a difference, looking up and seeing it. But I've never been so cold. We were tightly packed like penguins against the Arctic wind, but there's only so much body heat human beings can give off on a late November evening when the temperature drops close to zero.

I didn't think I could concentrate on anything except Katya, but Flame and I had to think of something, just to stop freezing solid, and just to get through the minutes that felt like hours and the hours that became even darker. We played word games, stupid ones. Dad even did whale jokes, but that's Dad for you.

"Where does a whale get its train ticket?"

"I don't know," said Flame, to humour him. "Where does a whale get a train ticket, Steve?"

"At the whaleway station."

"Can we do jokes about other things?" I asked.

"Bad taste as well as bad joke," said Dad, pulling a face. "Sorry, Daise." He was messing about, pulling bad boy grimaces, but then he became serious for a minute so I had to let him know he was forgiven.

He wasn't serious for long.

"Who do you call if you want to catch a whale?" he began, adding that he'd just made this one up, so I groaned.

"Net work whale!" he cried. "Net....to catch...?"

I glared at him this time and we did change the subject. Kyle and Dad ended up talking about big things like relationships, and how they'd messed them up. They didn't say much. It wasn't like *Eastenders*. They were editing because we were there, the sentences short and soft. But I didn't want to listen.

"Flame," I said, "How long did it take you to get used to it, when your parents split up?"

He took a long time to answer.

"About as long as you," he said.

"I'm not used to it yet."

"I know, but you will be."

I believed him, or part of me did. I knew he liked his step-dad. Flame liked everybody and I wished I was more like him. And more like he thought I was.

"You got used to having no hair," he said, as if it was a great achievement, the kind of thing that gets you a star on the wall at school, after it's been read out in assembly.

I didn't say anything. I didn't know if it was true. I knew I didn't want to think about it, didn't want being bald to be the thing I did best.

"I want to be Daisy who can dance," I said, "or Daisy who's good with words. Daisy who cares about the planet. Not the girl with no hair." I paused. "Not even the girl who's used to it."

It was his turn not to say anything for a moment. The dads were quiet now and I wondered whether they were listening. Suddenly the water and the engine sounded louder.

"Sorry," said Flame.

"No!" I cried. "I didn't mean that. I don't want you to be sorry."

He'd never been sorry for me. It was one of the things I loved about him. He was proud of me and it made me proud of myself.

"You are," he said, "you're all those Daisies. Crazy Daisy. A whole chain of Daisies."

I smiled. Our smiles were getting harder to see. We were a long way down the river now. We must be close. Surely...

Jamie was monitoring again. Breathing no better. Why would it be? Why wouldn't Katya be in massive distress, panicking inside that great still body? She was strapped down and helpless. She didn't know we were trying to save her life.

I didn't know the river could be so quiet and dark. I didn't know there were places along it where there were more trees than houses and more birds than people. In summer afternoon sunshine it would have been a holiday. Now it felt end-of-the-world-ish, cut off, adrift.

I hadn't been anywhere near Margate and neither had Flame. We thought of ice cream and beach huts and funfairs. But we never knew whether our guesses were right because all we saw was the coast, with the lights set back, as we ploughed out beyond the estuary, and the water started to throw the sting of salt into our faces. Waves chopped around the two boats, the whale barge and our inflatable. We were at sea.

The rain was clearing, the cloud too. We could see stars, just a few. Flame pointed out Venus, brighter than anything else. But we knew that any moment now everything else would fall away but Katya, because the time was coming. She was going to be free. Free to swim right back into trouble again, if she chose. And free to die. But free, with the ocean ahead of her.

It was no easier to lift her off the barge than on to it. And the watching was just as hard, only our brains had to fill in gaps when our eyes couldn't see. A helicopter began to buzz overhead. There was agitation. Anger. The world was going to want to see this. We couldn't keep it to ourselves, could we? But some of the team were determined to try.

Katya was hard to outline now against the sea and sky. But the sounds were clues. The straining. The shouts. The tilts and heaves. I held Flame's arm tightly against mine. Dad's arm was round my shoulder. He was muttering Dad-type encouragement to Katya, daft things like "Get off your ass, kid!"

The moment she hit the water was strangely slow. No huge, dramatic splash to drown us all. It was more of a surge and glide, as if she was just a very large boat lifted carefully down in an attempt not to spill the contents. A boat with no engine, no power. She had no energy of her own. She was listless, no movement, no life.

Hardly a word was whispered. We listened. With nothing to see, we waited for the sounds that would tell us … something, perhaps everything. And the whale filled the silence then, not with the sudden life-beat of her fluke, not with the parting of water, but with singing. It was pale, and it wouldn't be much use

154

to therapists with clients on a couch wanting to feel better about anything. But it was different all the same. You couldn't hear the pain, not the way we had heard it before. She was glad to be here. She was exhausted, and she hadn't stopped feeling afraid, but she was glad.

Flame heard it too. I could tell. And everyone felt it then, because a cheer went up, not full throttle but lifting with relief. Of course some of the people were exhausted too. And it wasn't only the whale that hadn't stopped feeling afraid.

I wondered what it would look like from above, whether the cameras in the helicopter could light up the whale we had already lost, and follow her out to sea, because the waves told us that's where she was heading. The water told us she was swimming. Not strong. Not fast. But pushing her great tired body through the sea.

A gush of wet breath shot from Katya's blowhole, through the quietness into the night, scattering, fading. Stopwatches were timing, waiting for the next. And then it came, fainter, less of a waterfall and more of a shower. But only because it came from further away. She was gathering pace. I heard the word 'momentum'. She was leaving us behind.

The rain had almost stopped. We waited, listened, shivered, and breathed out as if we hadn't breathed for hours.

"All right, then," said Dad, very quietly. "Time to go home."

"Like her," I said.

"Let's hope so," he said, in his voice that meant I'm only a child and he has to go along with my stupidity but he knows better. I knew he was right. I knew we hadn't seen a great Hollywood happy ending. And I had listened very hard for the other songs, for the sound of her mother and the others, all gathering to guide her and care for her, but I knew she was still alone.

It was the latest night of my life, by the time Dad had thawed me out and driven me home. Mum cried, and that made me cry too. Neither of us could have said why. Dad slept in the spare room because she insisted on him staying, but he was gone early in the morning to beat the traffic.

I didn't go to school. I slept. I had bad dreams of crowds of massive whales, surging and forging around a small one, nudging her and singing. But she was dead. And I wished I believed in happy endings the way I used to. I didn't even dream them any more. And I felt ashamed, because I wished I'd dreamed her leaping as high as the others, arcing across the moon.

There was no more in the news that next evening. I listened at six, then seven, but nothing. Just the same old "no more sightings …" Next morning, when I went downstairs, I heard it again. I told Mum I didn't want to know.

"Turn it off," I pleaded.

Mum turned off the radio.

"Daisy," she said, "sometimes you have to let things go."

I nodded. It was time I got ready for school.

Chapter Fifteen

At primary school Christmas is well underway by the end of November. It has to be, if plays are going to be rehearsed, corridors decorated and cards designed and made. In Mrs Young's class we were making a giant advent calendar so we had to be ready to open the first window in ten more days. Things were starting to get noisier and more colourful, and the hall was beginning to look more like a theatre, with a stage and lighting.

But Christmas made way for a sperm whale that Monday morning, because some of the teachers had seen me on television and knew I'd been one of the first to see Katya near Putney Pier. Mr Ogabe asked me to tell the school all about it in assembly, so I did, even though I hoped people weren't going to get sick of the sight of me up at the front with a microphone pointed at me. He didn't know I'd been there in the evening, when she was lifted, or that I'd been in the boat that followed her to the sea, and I didn't say. I don't know why. I kept it to myself, like a secret that would spoil if everyone heard it.

In class Mrs Young had us all researching whales in books and on the internet, and calculating how much longer and heavier one might be than another. We worked out that a Blue Whale wouldn't even fit on the bottom playground and people spent a lot of time with their mouths open saying things like "Wow!" and "Awesome!" We drew different whales to scale, one per cent of the real size, one centimetre to every metre. Even Kevin seemed to be finding maths cool.

At playtime he asked me if I'd like to be a sperm whale.

"Yes, in a way," I said, "if I was safe and free." I paused, and looked him in the eyes. "Why, Kevin? Are you going to tell me I look like one, because we're both bald and ugly?"

He looked away and over the fence.

"No," he said, in a small murmur.

"Good," I said, "I'm glad. Because I think sperm whales are amazing."

He didn't answer. I walked off briskly, as if I had somewhere to be. I half-expected rude things to follow and was ready to let them bounce off my back, but they didn't.

And then I saw George, pretending to be stuck in the play tunnel with his head grinning out at the front. A few of the little ones were laughing. Others were watching warily in case he turned into something fierce.

"You're back," I said, as he saw me and managed to ease himself free.

"Not for long," he said. "We're moving."

"Don't!" I cried. "It'd be my fault."

He shook his head. We were wandering around the playground now, but he wasn't looking at me.

"Wouldn't," he said. "Trouble and me, we always go together in the end. Like fish and chips. Only difference is, this time I did it for a good reason. More of a vigilante than a thug." He kicked a plastic pony that happened to be at his feet. "Well, bit of both."

"You're my friend," I said, weakly. "I'd miss you."

"You don't need a bodyguard any more, Daisy Waterhouse. You've changed. You got that boy licked."

George didn't seem to like that idea and his tongue poked out, as if he needed to get rid of a nasty taste in his mouth.

"You don't need to get into trouble," I said. "You could change too."

"Yeah," he said. "I wish. But then, my mum thought she could change my dad. It didn't work. He got worse." He sighed, and looked at me with a face I hadn't seen before. "I don't want to be like him."

"You're not!" I told him. "You're not cruel like Kevin. You don't want to make people cry. You tried to help me feel better when nobody else cared about my feelings."

He smiled. It was a small smile at first, but it grew steadily and his eyes came in on it too.

"I did, didn't I?"

"Yes!" I grinned.

"Cool!" he nodded away.

He asked me to tell him more about the whale, so I shared it all. He listened without saying a word, apart from long gasps and noises that got louder as the story progressed.

"So we'll never know," he said, at the end.

"No," I said, "probably not."

"And you'll never know whether I can change."

I pointed out that we could email. He said his mum had no computer. I said we could talk on the phone but he said he wouldn't be allowed, because of the bills.

"I might find you, though, one day," he said, "standing out in the crowd as usual." He grinned. "Dancing on stage at Sadler's Pond."

"Sadler's Wells," I said, smiling.

"And if I haven't changed by then I'll ask you to marry me," he said, "and see what you can do. You'd do it, if anybody can."

I couldn't help wondering how loudly Tamsin would squeal if she heard about that. My first proposal. Sort of. I felt myself begin to blush, and George laughed at me.

"Trouble is," he said, "I'd have to join the queue. And I don't mean for tickets."

That time I really did blush. I wanted to hug him, really. Instead I told him about the wedding that was coming up the next Saturday and said he could come if he wanted. Liz wouldn't mind.

"We'll be gone by then," he said.

"Who's we?" I asked. "Do you have any brothers or sisters?"

I knew there weren't any others at the school, but he'd never said. He didn't answer straight away, and something passed across his face that I didn't recognise. He looked at me, and his mouth opened, but nothing came out. Then he looked down at his feet and kicked one with the other.

"Something else you'll never know," he said, and ran.

Rehearsals went well that week. Well, mostly. Some of the witch's wolves were not as fierce as they should have been, which was funny because they included Kevin and Yaz. In one of the dances Mrs Young wanted them to kneel so that I could rest on them in turn, one hand and one foot, arm raised in evil threat. The music was wild rock from Mrs Young's teens, starting slow and queenly and becoming frenzied with fury. I loved it. But in Aslan's death scene, when the ghouls swirled on to help me tie him fast, the guitar music was Jimi Hendrix and all the boys watching had trouble keeping their heads from swaying and their arms from playing chords in the air. It was so powerful and so sad that when I plunged the knife I had to act really hard. Of course, being the baddie I got those just desserts Dad talks about in the end, and Aslan came back to life and breathed flesh and blood back into all the stone statues. I knew Mum was going to cry her eyes out.

By Wednesday George had gone, just like he said, with no proper goodbye, unless you count the wave he gave me, with his great wide back turned, as his class walked out of assembly the day before. Of course I don't know it was for me, but I'm claiming it. Mum asked Mrs Young for his address, even though she said he might already have moved.

I wrote a letter after school that day and Mum and I used that fold-up map to find out where the house was. We walked round just after dusk, and had trouble, in spite of the map, finding the house itself. When we finally decided we must be there, even though there was no number to help us identify the house, Mum insisted on walking my letter to the door. I don't know what she thought might happen, but it did look the kind of front garden where a rabid dog might leap the fence and go for your throat. It was cluttered with rusting metal trapping newspaper that flapped in the wind.

Mum scuttled back safe and sound, but she didn't see what I saw – a large face at the downstairs window, sandwiched between drawn curtains, staring at me. It was a full moon face, wide and blotchy, with a deep forehead and wobbly chins. I thought at first it was a woman, so it must be George's mum, but she wasn't the one I remembered and anyway, there was something in her eyes that wasn't old enough. Then she lifted to the window a plastic object in her hand, something she wanted to show me. In her thick arm she held a battered old Barbie, all matted blonde hair and boobs, and she smiled. She was a child, an enormous child. It was hard to guess her age, but she must have been old enough, at least, for Year One. She was trying to slip tiny kitten-heeled shoes onto the two centimetre feet, but they fell off as she waved at me.

George had a sister. One who never came to school. But then if her legs were as wide as her arms, she'd have an exhausting time putting one in front of the other. I guessed, as I smiled back at her, that she might have other reasons to stay away. And that her family might have reasons for wanting to keep her there.

Mum hadn't seen. The curtains pulled tight as she reached me and we started to walk home.

I was quiet and she knew something was up. Somehow I felt I'd seen something – someone – I wasn't supposed to see, that I was in on a secret no one had chosen to share. But that wasn't the only reason I was silent. I was searching for words that weren't harsh and cruel and Kevinish. And the only one that hung around in my head was the one I'd heard on news items about overweight people, how many there were and how worried the government was about them. Obese. That's what George's sister was. It was a technical and medical word, but 'massive' would have done. Only it wouldn't have been any kinder.

I thought about her a lot over the next few days, but I didn't hear from George. I knew he'd get my letter, though, and I was sure he'd be glad. I suppose it made me think about being me, and how it wasn't so bad, or as difficult as it had sometimes felt, deep down somewhere I didn't like to go.

It wasn't just at school that things were busy. Liz got married the next Saturday and I woke up feeling glad about being a part of it. Because Flame didn't come, Liz wondered whether Nina might like his place, and she was really excited because she'd never been to a British wedding. She sat in church with Mum and Kay and Tamsin while I followed Liz down the aisle. I didn't feel awkward or worried about being on show at the front of the church, with no bridesmaid's hair to curl or tie up or decorate. I just enjoyed it all: the splashed, blending colours of the dress, with its shine and rustle and spread, the little shiny pumps and the soft little matching cap that fitted perfectly around my head with its sequins and tiny mirrors. I didn't trip over, or drop my flowers, and I didn't even wonder whether anyone felt sorry for me or thought anything about anything.

Liz announced to everyone that this particular bride was going to make a speech even though traditionally it's the men who do the talking. There were lots of shouts back that it was no surprise.

"Today wouldn't have been the same without my bridesmaid Daisy Waterhouse," she said, right near the beginning, pronouncing my surname in that lovely Scottish accent that made it sound like the best name in the world. "She's an absolute star and a cracker and I love her to bits." She raised her glass then, "To the best bridesmaid in the history of matrimony!"

Then she handed over to the groom, her new husband, who'd already been really nice to me and told me I looked fabulous. Now, in front of all the tablefuls of guests, he said he'd heard what a good mover I was and he hoped I'd save a dance for him.

"Don't do it, Daisy!" shouted someone who looked like his brother. "He'll tread on every one of your toes!"

But I did, and we laughed all the way through. I don't even remember why. Nina, Tamsin and I practically never sat down. Well, Nina took a lot of food breaks, and ate Tamsin's wedding cake as well as her own. She'd never had British wedding cake before either. Mum had a good time too, and danced with

Matthew. I kept an eye on how close they got, and where he put his hands, but he was well-behaved (I suppose choirmasters have to be) and I liked the happy way he looked at her. And the way she looked back.

I didn't mind that Flame didn't come to the wedding in the end. I knew he had his own life to live, and it turned out that Fliss was in trouble with the law again. A new motorway was due to be built near where they lived and she was protesting, by lying down in the car park outside City Hall, where the Mayor worked. Of course she wasn't the only one, but she was one of the organisers and when the officials couldn't move their cars at the end of the day without running Fliss and the others over, the police asked them to move, but they all refused. Fliss got dragged off, and her photo was in the papers, trying to hold her ground while police officers grabbed her arms. Flame went with Kyle to the police station to collect her after she'd been charged with causing a disturbance.

Soon November gave way to December and I gave way over Christmas, first with Dad. He was practically bursting with excitement about getting a tree, and insisted on decorating the flat with tinsel and lots of tasteless Santas, Rudolfs and bells. Mum and I were in less of a hurry. We saved it up, and kept it low-key. Just a few stars on windows and doors, which we painted ourselves with peel-off silver and gold. They looked great at night.

There was Christmas shopping to do, of course, and Mum and I went one evening with Kay and Tamsin. The two of us got the mums to sit down in the café part of the store while we chose their presents secretly. Tamsin spent ages looking in the jewellery section, ooing and aahing and describing things as sooooo cool and sooooo pretty. She asked the assistant if she could have a look at the bangles standing in slots in a velvet tray. Then she kept changing her mind and asking me what I thought.

"Oh, actually," she said, really politely, "would you mind getting that other tray out so we can have a look at those too?"

And while the lady reached down into the cabinet to lift it out, she snatched a green stone bracelet out of its slot and slipped it into her pocket. I couldn't believe it. But I didn't have

163

the chance to do or say anything because then she was examining the second tray and oohing and aahing again.

"Actually," she said, "I'll leave it. Thanks."

And the lady didn't even look grumpy about all the time she'd wasted. She just said she hoped Tamsin would find something nice for her mum and there were some great bargains in the perfume section.

We were just turning to walk away. Something made me do it. I had to.

"Oh, look, Tammy!" I said, loudly, even though I never called her that, and I pointed to her pocket, even though nothing was showing. "That green bracelet must have got caught up with your sleeve!"

She froze. Then she felt inside, and said, "Oh! How did that happen?" and handed it over to the assistant, who took it, looked at me, looked at Tamsin and then said "Thank you," which was definitely for me. I don't know whether she knew. I think she had an idea. But she just said "Happy Christmas" again and the two of us left the section, me a few steps ahead of Tamsin, eager to find the mums and go home.

"Why did you do that?" she asked, as soon as we were into a crowd. Her mouth was down in a pout. "Mum would have loved that bracelet."

"Then go back and buy it," I said.

"I hate you," she muttered into her sparkly scarf, but she didn't sound angry. She sounded as if she might cry.

"I had to stop you," I said. "Sometimes you have to stop things or they just get bigger and bigger and worse and worse."

She didn't say a word. She just examined her fingernails and played with her rings.

"Why do you do it?" I asked. "You've got lots of money. Nina can't afford anything for her mum for Christmas. She's making something they demonstrated on Blue Peter, but she hasn't got all the bits yet." I paused. "But don't go being helpful by getting them from the stock cupboard."

Tamsin managed a half-smile although I wasn't really joking. She didn't say why. I don't think she knew.

"Fliss breaks the law," she said, suddenly, throwing it at me as if it would catch me out, bowl my stumps flat or something.

"That's not the same," I said. "She believes in things. She's trying to change the world. It's for a cause."

"My dad says the law is the law," said Tamsin.

"I don't think it is," I said. "What about Nelson Mandela and apartheid?"

Tamsin didn't know about South Africa and how the laws were unjust to people who weren't white until Nelson Mandela came out of prison and became President and changed them. She listened.

"Okay," she said, but I wasn't sure what she meant.

"You won't do it again?" I asked.

"No," she said. "I'm bored with it anyway. I'm bored with everything."

I sighed. I did feel, at that moment, a bit bored with Tamsin, but then she looked sad instead of moody and I felt sorry for her, even though I didn't know why.

Then I realised that she wasn't happy. And that being pretty, with gorgeous hair and all the clothes and accessories you want, and a perfectly white kitten, doesn't make you happy, even if your parents haven't split up and you know what's happening at Christmas.

"Shall we find some perfume for your mum?" I asked, and she nodded. We chose something, she paid for it, sprayed herself with it and cheered up a little.

And then I noticed that when we joined the mums in the café, mine gave me a big smile and Kay didn't even stop talking to look in Tamsin's direction. And I knew that was something I'd seen before, again and again.

That was just the start of the Christmas shopping, and I did some of it with Dad too, but he just couldn't wait to get out of each shop the moment we'd squeezed in, so I suggested that he get Oxfam Unwrapped presents like donkeys and seeds and he jumped at the idea. He's hopeless at presents anyway because he always left all that to Mum.

They told me around then that they'd been talking, and I did wonder ... Well, apparently children always do. But I didn't really think they were going to announce that they were getting back together, just like they'd announced that they were splitting up. In any case, that wasn't the idea. In fact there were lots of ideas and I was supposed to pick one.

"We've had an invitation, all of us, to spend Christmas Day with Fliss and Kyle and Ian and the boys and their cousins. And the world and his wife, really," said Mum.

"But it's up to you," said Dad. "Of course we can go to your gran and gramps. Or they can come here ..."

"With Grandma and Grandad."

I must have looked like a contestant on a quiz programme who hasn't got a clue and all the big money is hanging in the balance.

"I don't know," I said.

"Okay," they both said, separately. "Think about it." But I didn't really want to.

"We're looking forward to Narnia," said Dad, chirpily. "Can't wait."

"And we're not the only ones," said Mum, smiling, but I didn't ask. I didn't even wonder, really. I was looking forward to it too, but as far as Christmas was concerned, there didn't seem to be a solution.

I had an itchy White Witch wig from the fancy dress shop. It was long and jet black and very dramatic when my face was covered in white face paint and my lips were ruby red. It was when Mum was practising using double-sided tape to keep it on my head so that it couldn't fall off in the performance that she suddenly stopped. I could almost hear her breathing. The wig was in her hand and she was staring at the top of my head.

"Daisy," she said, "have you looked lately?"

I'd told her I never looked, but she wanted me to go to the bathroom with her. And there, in the mirror, we saw a cluster of very short, stubbly hairs, the kind you find on the cartoon chins of baddies. And another. And another. My follicles were taking a bit of long-overdue exercise. Mum started to cry, and apologised. I didn't mind her getting emotional because I knew how much she wanted my hair to grow back, but I couldn't let myself count on anything. I looked away, and asked her not to tell Dad, or anyone.

"It could be the start, darling," she said, and hugged me.

"Mmmm," I said, but I wished I hadn't seen and didn't know. I would rather have woken up one morning with fabulous shiny curls down to my shoulders.

Now the dreams started. The dreams of beautiful hair, and jagged, hay-like hair, and white fluffy old lady hair in a cloud-shaped cap. And hair that slid from my scalp that ran down the plughole like a river rushing to the sea. I was better off without them.

Our school production was on Friday afternoon and evening that week. In the matinee there were a few hitches. The boy Tamsin liked was in charge of CDs and had us all waiting in position for ages while he tried to get the machine to play. Then at last the music began. But. no one knew how *Baa Baa Black Sheep* came to be in that CD tray. And one of the ghouls in Aslan's death scene accidentally had her tunic tucked in to her knickers. If the mums were mostly too polite to giggle, a lot of the boys weren't.

But Mrs Young said that after that everything was bound to be perfect in the evening, and as far as I was concerned, she was right. It was. Mum hadn't said anything, and I'd forgotten the little hint about people looking forward to the show, so when we all walked in to the hall I got a really great surprise. There between Mum and Dad was Flame, his thumb up and his face split by a grin. As my smile faded slowly at the side of the stage I felt a tickle of nerves, warm and dry, even though the night was freezing and my legs and feet were bare. But I knew I was going to be the best I could be.

My dance with the wolves had never been so dramatic and at the end of it there was an enormous round of applause. A toddler had to be taken out sobbing when Aslan died but Mum admitted he hadn't been the only one in tears. At the end of the show the cheers were deafening and I knew we'd done well because Mrs Young looked pink and bright-eyed and overwhelmed.

"Twinkletoes! You were incredible!" cried Dad, and his voice almost bounced.

"Wonderful, darling," murmured Mum.

Flame gave me both thumbs now, his mouth tight as if words weren't enough.

"What are you doing here?" I asked him, and he touched my cheek because I was glowing and he wanted to borrow a bit of heat.

"Staying overnight," said Flame.

"We're both sleeping on your spare room floor," said Dad. "I've told him he'd better not snore."

"YOU snore!" I laughed. "You're like the Space Shuttle taking off!"

I felt happy. Mrs Young gave me a hug and Nina and Tamsin weren't the only kids who said I was good, but that wasn't it. Not all of it, anyway.

We had a brilliant weekend, and it felt like Christmas now. Flame and I talked and talked. We re-ran Katya, the whole story, because I think we wanted to hold on to the details and not forget. I told him about George and Tamsin and somehow everything made more sense. We understood why George had defended me and, maybe, why Tamsin stole. Understanding people helps. Flame said it's not always so easy to understand ourselves. And Kevin had us both beaten. But there must be reasons for the way he was. I decided I was tough enough now to find out. But whatever they were, I wasn't sure I was big enough to forgive him.

We wrapped presents and made cards and even licked a lot of old-fashioned paper chains. And after Dad left we went out on a freezing winter picnic with Mum and Matthew, but the sun shone on the last of the frost and the spiders' webs were jewels. We went swimming too, but I made sure Flame didn't see my bare head before I pulled my cap on, because it wasn't so bare any more.

There was a special service at Mum's church on the Sunday. Flame said he'd never been to church but he didn't mind trying it. It was called Christingle and I know the orange with all the bits stuck to it represented the earth, and the candle stood for Jesus, the light of the world. I was a bit nervous that some of the tiny children were going to drop their candles or set light to one another's hair, but they looked really pretty with the lights off. As for God, I wasn't sure whether he existed or if it made a difference whether he was real or only in people's heads. I knew he was in Mum's and she seemed glad about it.

"Bit mad," said Flame, when I asked him what he thought of the service, but he didn't seem to think that was a bad thing. I was sorry when he had to go, but we said we'd see each other over Christmas, one way or another.

So it would have been a great weekend. Later I happened to be cleaning my teeth at the basin while Mum knelt over the bath. All her hair piled on to the top of her head, where the water and shampoo kept it stiff like a dark ice cream whip. And I saw. The patch was big. It was just like mine had been, and she didn't know it was there.

I didn't say anything. I couldn't. In fact I started to wonder whether I'd really seen it, because once her hair was dry no one would have guessed. It looked as thick as ever. But when I lay in bed that night, I couldn't stop thinking about it. She'd been so much happier. I couldn't remember the last time she'd cried in the evenings. She felt at home in the house now and she'd sold a few more paintings. And she had the church, and Matthew too. I sometimes heard her talking to him on the phone, and I knew he came round to see her sometimes when I was at school. So why was her hair falling out when she was starting to like her life again? And what would he think if she ended up like me?

I know now that people always ask why God allows bad things to happen, and I know that as bad things go, alopecia is a doddle, a breeze, a walk in the park. But that night in my diary I wasn't thinking like that.

Why, I wrote, *would God, if there is one, do this to Mum?*

Chapter Sixteen

I didn't say a word to Mum, not for more than a fortnight. I watched, though, and checked. I studied her hairbrush, and it was clogged. I pulled the hairs out from the bristles and threw them away, hidden in tissue, just the way I used to do with mine. But they were her hairs and it was her brush. Didn't she look at it? Hadn't she seen?

And then I realised. She had. She knew exactly what was happening. But she wasn't going to tell me, not now, not until Christmas was over, not until she had no choice. I wondered whether she'd told Auntie Sue, or Liz, or Kay, but I suspected she hadn't. They would have been round. The door would have been tightly shut. There would have been empty wine bottles to recycle.

Maybe she hoped it would stop. The hair was having a wobble, that was all, a little blip, like a chin sprouting a spot. It would get back on track. After all, what were the chances of two bald females under forty living in one two-person family?

Meanwhile, one of those people was a lot less bald. My hair was growing steadily, and the plug hole after Mum's shower wasn't the only thing I was examining daily. I kept my head well covered when anyone else was around, even Dad. I didn't want any rumours going around the school. And once term finished, I didn't want Tamsin getting excited and counting, measuring or keeping a chart on her bedroom wall. I was doing all those things for myself, except that the chart was in a drawer. Private.

Mum looked too, of course, and she was happier every day. Too happy. It would have felt that way even if things had been different for her, but then if they had been, maybe she would have registered a notch or two lower on the emotion dial. Maybe the tears would have flowed less freely.

"Mum," I told her, a few days before Christmas, when the stubble on my scalp was dark enough to show in morning light, without electricity to point a finger, and she clasped her hands as if she was praying, because she couldn't speak for a moment and her eyes shone, "OTT!"

"I can't help it," she said in the end, holding on to me. "I'm just so glad."

And I would have been glad. Of course I would. But I never asked to hand over my problem to someone else, like that buck (whatever a buck is) that the politicians get accused of passing on because they haven't got the guts to hold on to it and deal with it. She put the kettle on, and I heard her singing a church song, very quietly under her breath, with a catch in her voice. I saw her, looking out through the window above the kitchen sink, and I couldn't bear it, because she hadn't seen the back of her head that morning, and I could. The skin was showing. The secret was out, and she didn't even know.

I ran upstairs and shoved myself back into bed. I told myself it was the cold unheated air driving me down like a fox into its hole, and closed my eyes as if the image of the scalp spreading out into her hair would go away. I felt my own head on the pillow, no longer silky smooth, and I felt angry. I can't explain it. It felt so wrong, and unfair, such a bad solution I couldn't imagine how anyone would think it worked. And then I heard her in the shower, and I wanted to bury my head so that I couldn't picture what might be washing away with the shampoo. And in my mind her head shaped small and hairless and alien and much too young.

The water gushed to a sudden stop. I can't describe the noise she made. It was almost silent, not a noise at all, more of a pause. I recognised it; I knew what it meant.

In the shower she was looking thin and cold, her arms around herself. At first she didn't see me, because she was looking at the curling thickness floating in the foam like streaking blood, but dark. So much hair. And then, whether she reached down to collect it because she saw me and was trying to stop me seeing, or because she was trying to stop the plug hole getting blocked, I don't know, but she was on her haunches, grabbing. And I couldn't bear it. It was as if everything gathered inside me in one rush and heaved itself out in a sob.

"No!" I cried, and I gave her a towel, leaned over and caught the hairs in my own fingers, but I was crying now and that made it hard to win.

"Daisy, leave it," she said, and her voice was too quiet. "Let me."

I didn't answer this time. I just kept trying to collect all the hair, but it was escaping and catching around the plug hole, or separating into strands that clung to the wall of the bath. I felt like a sandcastle up against the sea, or the child who built it, ankle deep in water. Tearful and red-faced with helpless heat.

Mum was wrapped in the towel now, a small turban around her head. I was still kneeling when I felt her arms round me, lifting me to my feet.

"Never mind the hairs, darling. Come on. Come on."

I let her pull me up and hold me. The cold room was steaming now. My face felt hot, my cheeks stinging.

"It doesn't matter," she whispered. "Don't worry."

I pulled apart from her, from the gathering heat of her, from the calmness that made me tight and tugged.

"You told God, didn't you? You did a deal! You prayed for this! You said, I remember. You said if only it was you! If you could swap you would, my hair for yours!"

My hands were in fists and they wanted to beat her. But they lay still and curled on her shoulders, and my head went down. I didn't want to look at her. I knew I was shouting rubbish, ridiculous childish nonsense, and yet somewhere inside me it made such perfect sense because she would do it. If God would go along with it, she'd give up more than that. Hair! It was nothing! It was the least any mother could do.

I looked up from her shoulders and tried to fix on her eyes, tried to hold them, make her see, make her answer. But she wouldn't look back. She wasn't speaking. She wasn't shaking or crying either, but she didn't want to look at me and she didn't want to speak. Except in the end to murmur my name, just my name.

"Did you?" I cried, not so much an accusation as tiredness now. Because she wasn't denying it like I'd waited for her to do. And I'd expected the denial, firm and reassuring, to come straight back at me. Instead she gave me nothing but silence and eyes that wouldn't connect with mine.

And I knew she'd offered. She'd done it for me. But she hadn't asked me if that was what I wanted, and I would have said no.

"Yes," she said. "I prayed. A bit late in the day. I did ask. People ask God for a lot of stupid things, but this isn't one of them. I wanted to take it over, my turn now, so you don't have to carry it any longer."

I stared.

"But that's like an old, old story from when people didn't know things! How can it work like that? How can you ask? And why would God do it? Why didn't He tell you not to be stupid?" I stopped. The words were too fast and too breathy. They ached. "Tell Him you didn't mean it. Please!"

"Daisy," said Mum, "listen. Listen to me."

Her voice had changed. It had thickened, deepened, risen. It was her strong voice and I knew already what she was going to say. I could have said it for her, but I didn't want to hear it.

"All I know is that I prayed. It's happened. I didn't expect it to, but it has. I don't know why or how. I don't even know for sure that there is a God at all, or that if there is, He even listens, never mind intervenes."

I didn't know what she was saying and I realised she didn't know either.

"But there is no deal. Daisy, if deals were possible, don't you think I'd have done one long ago? We'd all be negotiating twenty-four seven! But what kind of God would we be dealing with?" She paused. "Sir Alan Sugar?"

I snorted, and she had to grab some toilet roll for my nose as well as my eyes.

"So it's not your fault! Nothing is! And your hair is growing back and I'm delirious. I want this. I'm glad."

"But you're almost happy!" I protested. "You're getting on with Dad and you're painting, and Matthew ..." I looked at her. I didn't know how to finish.

"Matthew?" she repeated, and I knew she was thinking it through, but I just wanted the truth. "I don't know what will happen with Matthew, Daisy, but if he cares for me less because I have less hair – or no hair at all – then he's not much of a man, is he? Not much of a loss."

I nodded, but I didn't want her hurt. I didn't want her outside the front door surrounded by people who might try. Or hurt her anyway, without trying at all.

"You ask about God and I don't know. Your dad thinks religion is stupid, pipe dreams, small comfort. Because so much is random. And maybe he's right, I don't know, but it's not what I feel. I feel I got lucky. I got what I wanted, deal or no deal."

Dad would have laughed and done a TV joke. I didn't feel like smiling. And she didn't seem to realise that mums are supposed to make sense.

"Maybe life is just happenings, with or without reasons, one thing leading to another, another just bursting out of nowhere, no warning, no cause. Accidents. Outcomes. It makes no difference. We have to deal with it anyway. You have. And thanks to you I can too. I will."

"But ..."

I could have begged her again, but I'd lost the thread. I was as confused as she was. I nodded instead. She could deal with it. Of course she could. And I remembered it was nothing. Just dead material. Follicles. Like fingernails. Nothing. Only the world didn't know that, got the scale wrong. Over-rated. Pride and glory. Beauty salons. Fashion magazines. The right image. And the wrong one.

And I wanted to save her from it anyway, just like she'd wanted to save me.

"I'm not pathetic any more," she murmured. "Honestly. I'll survive. I've got you."

I told her she had, but would she put some clothes on? And then when she came downstairs to the kitchen I'd made a pot of tea, so I poured her a mug and we talked about small things, even smaller than the hairs on my head. Needing bread. Putting the recycling out on a different day because of Christmas.

"Daisy," she said, "I'm so sorry about Christmas. What can we do? I wish…" and she stopped, because I knew there were many things, more than I could guess.

"Can't we do everything?" I said. "You and me, me and Dad, everyone. As long as we make it work, it will, won't it?"

So we drew up a schedule. Not one Christmas but lots of variations on a theme, from the two of us to a party.

And it worked, mostly, give or take the odd awkward silence and a few tears from Grandma. Because I told Dad he had to try. And Mum told her parents (I think Grandma was trying, until the sherries) and he told his. And then there was Flame and a Christmas noisier, spicier, wilder and wackier than anything I had ever imagined.

So I'll be starting at the comprehensive in September. Mum is engaged to Matthew, so I guess I'll be doing my bridesmaid bit again before long. Dad says he's playing the field (I heard him on the phone to Uncle Will) but I suppose it's a matter of time. After all, as he said, a head of hair like his is hard to resist.

In some ways the last year has been quiet. Sometimes things get churned up like a storm at sea and sometimes they settle. The wind drops. But I could handle a gale now and then, because there's no risk of hats blowing off and bobbing into puddles. My hair is down past my ears. It's still a free spirit, going off in all directions, and brushing and combing it is still like wading through the undergrowth and wishing you'd got a machete. And Dad has got a whole new repertoire of rude jokes like that one. It's my hair and I can live with it. But I could live without it too.

I do know it might fall out again, like Mum's. She lost it all, faster than me, and it hasn't grown back, not yet. What she did for me was try to make a sacrifice. She likes that word (and the Elton John song). It shouldn't have worked and it didn't work, but even though God isn't like that, the result was the same. She did it out of love and maybe it was the love that made it happen. We'll never know.

I think it's been harder than she imagined in lots of little ways. So I try to make it easier, and when the weather's warm enough and we go out together, I link arms and look proud of my bareheaded mum. Because I am. And so's Matthew.

Maybe it will come back in time for the wedding, but she knows it might not, and she says her smile will be just as big in the photos, with or without hairs on her head. She's a lot tougher than she used to be. And maybe I'll be a bald grandma or a bald teenager. But I'll be ready. And if that's the worst thing that ever happens to me or my world I'll be getting off, as Tamsin would say, soooooo lightly.

Liz had a miscarriage a little while ago, and Mum's been looking after her because although she hadn't planned on a baby at forty she'd got used to the idea as the baby grew inside her. It would have been called Ayr, whether it was a boy or a girl, because she grew up there, and because of the kind we breathe to live. Only it never did. She's back at work part-time, but wearing black, and no bangles. Mum and I made a card, but there wasn't much to say.

Nina has changed. She's much more confident now. In fact, she sang at the end of term concert, just after my dance, and her picture was in the local paper. Her English is better and she's turning out to be clever as well as really kind. Tamsin says her singing voice is weird, but she admits it's beautiful. The song she sang, with no accompaniment, was strange and wild and wave-like, and very sad. But when she'd finished it, the clapping turned to stomps and we all saw a smile she'd been hiding.

I'm still friends with Tamsin. Not best friends and never will be, but we get on. I won't see as much of her after the summer because her parents are sending her to a private school. At the end of that Christmas she told her mum she had stolen quite a few things from Harford Junior, things that belonged to Mrs Young, like a pen and a little decorated mirror that she had left on her desk. But she only confessed because she was determined it wasn't going to happen again, and I don't think it has. She's looking for something. That's what I think. Only she doesn't know what it is and maybe it's herself.

Tamsin has asked me more than once whether Flame is my boyfriend and I know she's a bit jealous because she thinks he's unbelievably cool. I try not to give her that look she gives me, the one that says, *you're sooooo weird*. But it's not like that with Flame and me. We're just closer than I thought I could ever be with any girl or boy. I read his mind. And then he says things I couldn't have dreamed. And does things I'd never think of doing. Mum says we'll end up together one day, and I just say "Mu – uum!" as if she's singing Eurovision songs in front of my friends (which has been known). But I don't really mind.

Mum's done a sketch of the two of us, Flame and me, but we're not in a heart or anything. Katya's there too, or a bit of her, because her back is bumping out of the water. It was my birthday present, on top of another drawing. They were both in pale wooden frames and wrapped in lilac tissue. The one underneath was familiar, but unexpected.

"Thanks, Mum," I told her, as I looked at the drawing of Dad. Complete and smooth. No gap teeth, no angry rip down the middle. The strokes were careful, the pencil soft. This Dad was so fresh and new, I could almost smell the almond and vanilla straight from the shower. I told Mum it was even better than the original.

They're both on the wall now, one each side of My Sweet Rose.

I've kept in touch with Jess. In fact I told her more than I planned to, in a letter that grew and grew, and she called me when it arrived. She didn't say much, and neither did I. We laughed a bit about things that weren't funny. But it was great to hear her, even though she sounds like someone from *Neighbours* now and I'm working on my impression of her saying "G'day Daise." She's still in Australia but they'll be moving back before long and I know we'll stay friends. So it's something else to look forward to.

I was School Council Rep this term: a landslide, Mr Ogabe said. It took me whole seconds to close my mouth. So we became a green school, recycling paper, cutting down on electricity, LEGGING IT as much as we could and starting a human chain so that younger children could join it instead of going in their mums' cars. It wasn't hard to make changes that meant something. We even won an award. It's harder to save the polar bears and some fights get tiring. But you can't give up. That's all I know for sure.

I haven't heard from George. But I haven't given up on that either. When I'm old enough I'll have a space online and try to find him. Someone will know. It's hard to disappear in a high tech world even if you want to, and he won't mind being found, not by me. I think about his sister sometimes, because some people whose names needn't be mentioned again might call her a whale. And she's beached in a different kind of way. But I bet if anyone can get her swimming, it's George. And maybe if I ever meet up with him, I'll get to know her too.

Flame and I talk about Katya. If she's out there, she'll still be a baby, still in her mother's sights, still growing, so much living to do, such huge depths to explore. We'll never know. Some things you never can. Some things you can't change however much you want them to be different. Some things you just hope for. And don't forget. Some things change you, maybe for ever.

So I'm not a Waterhouse girl. I'm me.